9/11/11

W9-CSZ-312

Happy
Birthday
Grant!

Love, Joe, Anna, Brendon
Miles & Henry

RIGHT OF WAY

RIGHT OF WAY

Stories

ANDREW WINGFIELD

Washington Writers Publishing House
Washington, DC

COVER PRODUCTION by Yvonne Cramer

BOOK DESIGN by Andrew Wingfield and Barbara Shaw

TYPESETTING by Barbara Shaw

LIBRARY OF CONGRESS CATALOGUING-IN-PUBLICATION DATA

Wingfield, Andrew, 1966-
  Right of way : stories / Andrew Wingfield.
    p. cm.
  ISBN 0-931846-94-3 (pbk. : alk. paper)
  1. African American neighborhoods—Washington (D.C)—Fiction.
  2. Gentrification—Fiction. I. Title.
PS3623.I6625R54 2010
813'.6—dc22
                                                2010018075

Printed in the United States of America

WASHINGTON WRITERS' PUBLISHING HOUSE
P. O. Box 15271
Washington, D.C. 20003

FOR TANIA
who brought me to the neighborhood
AND FOR SAM AND ABE
who came along and made it ours

CONTENTS

ACKNOWLEDGEMENTS

I WOULD LIKE TO THANK the Vermont Studio Center, the Banff Centre's Wired Writing Studio, and George Mason University for providing me with time to work on this collection. Annabel Lyon, a wonderful writer, read many of these stories at various stages and offered essential advice. If not for her keen ear and her tough questions, much of the potential in this material would have gone unrealized.

I would also like to thank the editors of the following journals, where versions of most of these stories first appeared: *The Antioch Review* ("Lily Pad" and "Goodbye"), *The Fourth River* ("Wonders of the World"), *Potomac Review* ("Heirlooms"), *Prairie Schooner* ("Air Space"), and *Terrain* ("Precious" and "The Hank Williams Dialogues").

Finally, my most profound thanks go to my family. My wife, Tania Karpowitz, inspires me continually with her dedication to her craft and the beauty of her paintings. The insight and compassion I see in her work set the standard I reach for in mine. Our sons, Sam and Abe, keep me limber in all kinds of ways, and remind me every day, several times a day, that stories are as necessary as food.

PRECIOUS

ACCORDING TO MY MOTHER, I am a gifted person who lacks the ability to focus. The truth is I focus very well on things that hold my attention. Like this dog that just passed the door of our restaurant and the woman who's passing the post office a block back, giving chase. Strange-looking dog: needle-nosed, bat-eared, with a collie-sized body and stubby dachshund legs.

This peculiar animal trots down the opposite sidewalk with a smile on its face. The woman is a block behind, yelling for the dog to stop. A large black woman, built to proportion unlike the dog—long legs and arms, ample everywhere. Her jeans are tight and her hightops aren't tied, which means the dog can hold its lead without trying too hard.

"PRECIOUS," the woman yells. "STOP NOW PRECIOUS. DON'T *MAKE* ME COME AFTER YOU."

No wonder the dog is smiling.

Left to my own devices, I would sit here behind the steering wheel and watch them pass, not leaving the car or entering the restaurant until after they vanished. A rich moment: late-spring evening, soft air, the street still damp from this afternoon's shower. A sleepiness in our little crossing, a few cars waiting for the light to change, a delicate, lemony scent descending from sidewalk locust trees, a faint odor of rot rising from the storm drains. And then this fabulous commotion.

But I am rarely left to my own devices. Harriet sits next to me and she wants to know what the woman is yelling about. In Cleave Springs, the cause of such shouting isn't always so benign. I point to the dog.

Harriet gets out of the car and penguin-walks into the Avenue. The woman has stopped in front of the plate glass window to the right of Depot's door. I expect her to yell again but instead she produces a big blue bandana from somewhere and begins to mop her brow—a large gesture, dramatic.

Harriet stops on the double yellow line and turns back to me. "Come on."

I see moments, Harriet sees situations. And this situation is tailor-made for us—an opportunity, in my wife's view.

Harriet gains the sidewalk and plants herself smack in the middle, to cancel any thoughts the woman might have about pursuing the dog further.

"That's your dog?"

The woman looks suspiciously at Harriet, as people sometimes do when she inserts herself directly into their business. Her eyes shift, scanning the sidewalk up ahead.

"My cousin's dog."

"Your cousin lives in Cleave Springs?"

The woman shakes her head. "Prince George's."

"We'd better catch that dog quick, then. It's lost."

Concern carves two deep lines across the woman's brow. "That girl, she'll *kill* me if something happen to Precious."

"Don't worry," Harriet says, turning back to make sure I'm on her flank. "We'll get Precious back. Won't we, darling."

"*We'll* sure try."

I could stick around to thank Harriet for giving me this chance to practice my chivalry, but that would increase the dog's head start. It would also delay Harriet's next move—the reassuring hand placed on the woman's shoulder, the invitation to come inside Depot. Harriet will seat her in one of the front tables, so she can see out to the street. She'll bring the woman a soft drink and make small talk to distract and calm her, create a human connection. By the time I return with the rescued dog, my wife will know the woman's story. Harriet will have built another bridge between New Cleave Springs and Old Cleave Springs, between us and one of the lifelong denizens of the neighborhood that we and our restaurant are helping to transfigure.

One problem: I'm not catching the dog. Oh, I'm trying. I'm running at a good clip, building momentum, warming to my task, but wily Precious is onto me. The dog runs with its tail straight back for aerodynamic efficiency. The bat-ears stand at attention. Every twenty or thirty seconds one of the ears twists back in my direction and the eyes follow for a quick confirmation. No matter how fast I go, Precious keeps the distance between us constant.

It doesn't hurt the dog's cause that I'm shod for the dinner rush—leather-soled loafers Harriet picked out to dress up my black jeans and my crisp blue shirt. No competent judge of such things would ever call me fit, but I was terribly fit at one time, a

punishing open-field tackler on the high school football fields almost two decades ago. My mother has noted that I am one of
those people who barely skim the surface of their own capacities
the vast majority of the time. Without trying, I hold a deep well
of energy in reserve. I am six-foot-two, with a fairly long stride.
For each step I take, Precious needs ten or so. Surely I can outlast
this dog.

If it takes a while, so be it. What an evening to be running
down the Avenue. Now is the transition time between work and
dinner. People are out. Precious and I weave among them. Gordon the attorney is locking up his office, but Emily the candle
maker will keep the shop next door open for another hour. Gordon waves at me and smiles, shifts his wire-framed gaze up the
Avenue in the direction of Precious. I smile too. A real smile,
mine. I like being known on the Avenue, even if it is a guilty
pleasure. My life here is a bitter pill my mother must swallow
every day. Poor Mother. She preferred it when I was known in
the powerful rooms whose doors my first wife opened for me.
It squared with her aspirations for me when I was still playing
politics across the river.

Mother was skeptical of Harriet's charms when they first
met, and utterly immune to the charms of Cleave Springs when
Harriet and I first moved here. It *was* a more rugged place back
then, yet Harriet and I fell for its cute old houses and gritty main
drag. America is a rich country growing poorer all the time in
places. Cleave Springs was a real place, a place that rose early last
century with the great railyard that spawned it and then declined
as the railyard went quiet. A place that had tasted death and was
waiting to be coaxed back to life.

By now the Avenue is rife with reclamations. Emily the candle maker, a mother of two, is recently out of the closet. Gordon the attorney is a refugee from some big Manhattan firm. I was a few months clear of the divorce when Harriet found me over in the nation's capital, still skulking and conniving with the rest of the hyenas on Capitol Hill. She plucked me from the wreckage of my first attempt at making a man's life, talked me into a version of myself that sounded sweeter than Mother's.

And here he is now, the reinvented me, a dutiful husband playing the role his wife has scripted, a decent citizen committing a useful deed, a novice restaurateur in jeans and loafers, dashing down one of the Avenue's better blocks. I follow Precious past the pottery studio, the custard shop, the yoga center, my body alive with the running, stimulated by the chase, for the first time chafing slightly at this costume's constraints. I undo the top buttons on my shirt, slip the cuffs open to admit some air.

And then Precious stops, veering into the bed of pansies that fronts the Thai restaurant.

"Is that all you've got," I tease, slowing to a walk. "I'm just getting warmed up, little dog."

"Hey Precious." I shift into my dog-soothing voice and squat at the edge of the flowers. "Why don't you take a whiff of this hand. Why don't you check me out a little."

The dog stands six feet from me panting rapidly, tongue lolling, tail brushing the barberry at the back of the bed. What ears! Each one is almost as large as the skull, broad at the base and curving up to a rounded tip. Soft and deep, a pair of big mitts made for fielding sounds. The nose is dark and sharp. The top lip is up off the teeth.

I move to narrow the gap between us and Precious snaps at me once before darting away. I rear from the dog's strike and note the sound of canine teeth clicking together. I take several quick strides, lunge for the retreating animal with both hands but grasp air only.

Up once again in a running posture, I continue down the Avenue's wide, shaded sidewalk. I'm running faster now, feeling freer than before. I'm glad to know that Precious isn't going to cave. I'm ready for a little competition, pleased somehow by this new hint of danger: the ivories are in play. What a relief to be out here, instead of back in the restaurant where I am still trying to fit. Harriet wasn't raised to this line of work either, yet she has taken to it. From dining room to kitchen to bar, she moves anywhere with a natural air of command—even more convincing since she's started to show.

I pick up the pace, welcome the sweat spreading down from my armpits and up from the small of my back.

Precious has plenty of go left in those stumpy legs. We're coming up to the Lily Pad, Cleave Springs' chief café, and though I probably know half the people at the outdoor tables I'm not looking for familiar faces now. I'm locked in on my quarry. I'm settling into a kind of deep, predatory patience. I've watched the nature shows, I know that wolves have more than just power and endurance going for them, I know it's their awful patience that really makes the difference. I'll catch this dog. I can wait.

The block beyond the Lily Pad is, as we say, *transitional*. The new tacqueria and a pair of antique stores face a sealed up storefront, a failing laundry, a soup kitchen where homeless men chase sermons with meals. Three times a day, they line up out front. It annoys Harriet, the careful way I study those fellows' faces whenever we happen to pass the line. How many new leases have been drawn on each of *those* lives?

Quit it, Harriet always says, *they're not you.*

Harriet. By now she and Precious' guardian are seated by the restaurant window, sipping cool drinks and talking. It's easy for me to imagine; Harriet conducts such conversations fairly often. Old Cleave Springs has been through hard times. If it's ready for anything, it's ready to talk. Most stories begin with the railyard, granddaddy worked in the yard, then daddy after him. Everything was good until the yard shut down and the families started unraveling—departures, foreclosures, addictions, arrests. Harriet listens with alarming interest: the more you tell her, the more she takes off your chest, the deeper your debt to her becomes.

Up ahead is the busy intersection where the Avenue crosses Joiner Road, the boundary between Cleave Springs and Brimslea. Precious speeds up as she nears the intersection, as if she's trying to time the light. Without breaking stride she plunges into the street and completes an immaculate crossing.

By the time I arrive the light in my direction couldn't be any redder; the pedestrian box offers an emphatic DON'T WALK. I don't walk, but run headlong into traffic, intent on losing no ground. A feast of honks and screeches. I slap a green front fender as if fighting off a would-be blocker. Foolish. Exhilarating.

When I gain the next curb I speed up to close the distance Precious picked up when the traffic broke my stride. I run hard for half a block, then settle back into my wolf-lope.

I'm content for Precious to run right through Brimslea. We'll have our showdown at some point, that's inevitable now. I'd prefer to cross the bridge over Ganders Run and get into Hillside, an upscale residential zone where no one is likely to be watching. But what if we extended this game of preferences, Precious fleeing with fuel enough to lead me out of Hillside and into the next neighborhood? And the next? For a heady minute I indulge this vision, Precious changed from quarry to guardian, a hairy angel leading me beyond Harriet's orbit, out past the pull of love and need and fear, into a weightless world where nothing at all is expected, a timeless black zone where no past can haunt you and no future can fall to pieces.

But Brimslea is no place for escapists; its vividness quickly hauls me in. The sidewalk here is even more crowded than back in Cleave Springs. Everyone is Salvadoran, a thriving legion of tough, diligent people doing the jobs most Americans don't want. One of these women will come to care for our newborn child in a couple of months. Some of these men humped the sheets of drywall and stacks of lumber, the wheelbarrows of brick and sacks of concrete that enlarged our tiny house and made it a fit place for the coming brood. Others mow our lawn, change our oil, wax our car, toil in our restaurant's kitchen.

Harriet has Spanish enough to chat up the Salvadorans who work for us, find out what town they come from, who's spending the money they send back home. But when I pass close by the men in the restaurant kitchen, they always go quiet. It's a certain kind of quiet—playful, ironic, watchful, a quiet that pokes all kinds of holes in my shaky performance.

As I weave amongst the people now I don't hear their voices, but feel them watching me, laughing silently at me and the absurd dog I'm chasing. I endure the strong fish odor that wafts out from the *Feria del Pescado*, briefly savor the smell of grilled meat and spices around *El Jardin*. Precious passes the check cashing place and the grocery, giving me reason to hope we'll continue along this end of the Avenue and clean out of Brimslea. But suddenly, for no reason I can detect, the dog swerves off across the lawn of an apartment complex.

I reach the lawn just in time to see Precious round the corner of a yellow stucco building. The grass in the complex is weedy and long. The stucco is moldy; brown paint peels from the trim. I follow Precious' path and find a kind of courtyard, walled on three sides by the yellow stucco buildings. Clumps of ratty crepe myrtle grow here and there. Lone males peer down from wide open windows two and three stories up. A sense of recent hush, as if my emergence on the scene has silenced a lively exchange. I slow to a walk and scan the courtyard for Precious.

The dog has taken up a position in the joint where two of the buildings meet, back under the foliage of a bushy yew. Precious in a corner, preparing for a last stand. I laugh at the High Noon drama of it and glance up at one of the young Salvadorans in his window, then another. I'm fishing for signs of humor or sympathy. Both men show me faces of stone.

I stand ten feet away from Precious, whose ribcage puffs rapidly. The lip is up off the teeth again, the tongue lolls, the eyes burn darkly. A defiant growl rises from the throat. As I unbutton my shirt I glance over my shoulder again. Faces appear in several more windows now: older men, a few women, children of all ages. I am the entertainment.

The shirt is heavy, wet to the touch. I wrap it tightly around my left hand. Thus equipped, I assume the wrestler's pose, knees bent, wrapped paw raised for defense. All these strangers' eyes upon me, yet it's Mother's gaze I feel most acutely. No, she can't see me now, but this is *how* she sees her only son. Exposed, displaced, misspent.

I lunge forward. Precious bounds to meet me, leaps at my throat and clamps fiercely on the swaddled hand I raise in her path. A sudden heat there, fangs piercing through layers of cloth and skin, probing deep enough to tap the dark energy that once guided me to all the sons who suffered my furious blows on the gridiron those long-ago Friday nights. As I did then, I yell like a barbarian now, loud and long, clutch the animal's haunch with my free hand and raise both arms high above my head, the squirming body splayed in my reaching hands like a child being offered up for sacrifice.

I turn a slow circle, staring back at the watchers, surveying my options. I could hurl the creature hard against the building, dash its brains out. I could lower it to my breast and bring it dutifully back. I could bend over, pry the jaws apart, and see to my maimed hand.

I am still completing my circle, still revolving my choices when I catch sight of Harriet and the woman, who didn't wait back at the restaurant after all, but must have trailed me all this way in the car. The woman halts the instant she catches sight of me, steps back as if I've pulled a gun. But Harriet continues toward me, impressively pregnant, moving with the determined air of a person intent on dispensing mercy or justice.

I have warned her before, but words only go so far. At long

last, she's forced to see the actual me: feet planted on the ground, legs spread apart, back straight, chest bare and heaving, sweat streaming down my body, blood beginning to trickle down one of my raised arms. She pulls up a couple of feet from me and studies me with great concentration.

"That's right," I say. "*I'm* going to be somebody's *father.*"

She nods.

"I'm wounded."

"I know," she says, stepping up close to me. She tips her head to the side and kisses me on the rib.

"Let go," she whispers, because she believes I eventually will.

HEIRLOOMS

D ALE HUBBARD lay headphoned on his couch, easing into the opening chapter of *Middlemarch*. It was Saturday. He had just returned from the library, bearing the hefty folder of discs with the tender urgency of a wine-lover approaching the dinner table, a rare vintage cradled in the crook of his arm. The voice of the reader—his reader—was balm in Hubbard's ears. He lay back and listened to her greedily, the volume a touch too high. He would turn it down after the opening chapter, or perhaps after chapter two—once this first fever had passed.

But after only a few paragraphs a flurry of knocks on the front door spoiled the whole event. Six small collisions of knuckle and wood. Crisp. Cheerful.

He pressed the pause button and went to the door with the headphones still on his ears. As soon as he opened it the woman's hand came at him. She introduced herself, pointing up the street toward the house she and her husband had recently finished reviving.

"I've met the whole block by now," she said, handing him a business card. "Except you."

Hubbard squinted at the card.

"That's the guy who removed the dead pine tree from our front yard. I think it was even taller than yours is. He's great, and super-reasonable. Has a lawn service too, I'm pretty sure."

Hubbard yawned.

"Just thought I'd give you that before your letter from the CSCA comes."

"Cleave Springs Citizens Association," she said in answer to his puzzled look. "Your property was on the agenda at the last meeting. That tree is kind of a safety hazard, don't you think? Hanging over the sidewalk the way it does."

That tree was a great dead honey locust that stood in Hubbard's side yard. The tree dated Hubbard. It had been very much alive five years before, when he and Leona first arrived in Cleave Springs. Back then the whole *neighborhood* had been a safety hazard. For the first wave of pioneers, danger was just part of the Cleave Springs experience.

Even in those days Cleave Springs was usually placid during daylight hours. But after dark, the pioneers holed up in their houses and yielded the streets to a large contingent of addicts and thugs. The right of way playground, up the street from Hubbard's place, functioned as an evening drug emporium. Dealers and customers commonly stopped into the corner store directly behind Hubbard's house for refreshment and sometimes settled their differences in the asphalt parking area adjacent to his driveway. Shattering glass and angry voices often punctured his dreams; gunshots woke him once in a while.

The old couple who lived on the chimney side of Hubbard's

house were retired teachers, a pair of staunch progressives. The two women who renovated the Cape Cod on the other side, across Early Street, belonged to Cleave Springs' bustling lesbian community. Hubbard himself had no pressing need for an alternative culture, no moral or political commitment to living amid blight. He just saw how much Leona liked the bungalow. On an early foray into the cramped attic she discovered a packing slip made out to a Franklin Peters, the home's original owner. The year was 1927. Mr. Peters had ordered the house from the Sears, Roebuck catalogue and the precut pieces had arrived on a freight car at the nearby railyard.

Leona framed that packing slip and hung it in the hallway. She spent a year outfitting the place with authentic furniture and accessories. At some point during that year she stopped using birth control and began to bring baby furniture home from antique stores and sales. Then she got sick; that is, she discovered she'd been sick quite a while already. Very sick. Hubbard spent the second year in Cleave Springs nursing Leona and began the third year there a widower, alone in a house he hadn't chosen, in a neighborhood of dubious security. But he didn't move, or even think about moving. To Hubbard, stasis *was* security.

For fourteen years now, each weekday from ten to two, Hubbard had hosted the midday program at the local classic rock station. He wore his hokey on-air moniker like an old costume whose elbows were about to blow. He used a stagy baritone to manufacture enthusiasm for songs with pull dates that had long since passed. He fielded phone calls from ditzy listeners and plugged performances by geriatric bands. A shy man, he refused to appear in public, as his colleagues often did to promote the station; but he pulled such solid numbers that the bosses didn't bother him. In the jock pit, Hubbard delivered the goods.

The patter he spoke into the microphone was a kind of verbal artifact, fashioned from phrases and intonations that had issued from the mouths of the hoodlums and stoners he overheard in the high school hallways back in the late 1970s. (Hubbard himself had been a nerd.)

Hubbard said things like, *Demon here, rockin you through the lunch hour. I'm featuring a* GREAT *band on today's Blue Plate Special. Stick around, I know you're gonna be stoked.*

He said, *Cool tune.*

And, *Cool tune*—VERY *cool tune.*

And, *It's gonna be a* GREAT *show—I'm all over this one, and you should be too. Hey, if you want to score tickets, don't even* THINK *about touching that dial.*

Hubbard couldn't imagine anything more excruciating than going to some big arena to hear a bunch of arthritic rockers travesty their old hits. His distaste for classic rock had grown extreme. He would sooner eat spoiled food than subject himself to a whole song by Boston or Blue Oyster Cult. Not that other kinds of music appealed to him greatly. About the only music that didn't repel him or leave him cold was the raucous gospel that poured forth every Sunday morning from the windows of Mt. Zion Church, which stood directly across the street from his front porch.

Except for those Sunday mornings, Hubbard listened to audio books. His taste in reading material was catholic, driven more by the voices of the readers he favored than by the content of the books. Once he fell for a reader's voice, he'd listen faithfully to whatever books that person had recorded. His all-time favorite was an English actress whose voice was rich and delicate, like the scent of locust blossoms. She specialized in nineteenth century novels by women. Hubbard had listened to all the major works of Jane Austen, George Eliot, and the Brontes—most of them multiple times.

He couldn't really remember what Leona's voice had sounded like. He had forgotten her smell. Her taste—her eye— he couldn't forget because his house reflected it from floor to ceiling. Little inside had changed during the three years following her death. Her clothes remained in the bedroom closet and drawers, her jewelry box on the dresser. Hubbard rarely ventured into that room. He moved the baby furniture from the house's other bedroom out to the garage, then brought his clothes in and stored them in the closet. On the futon he bought he would doze fitfully through the nights while one of his chosen voices poured sentence after sentence into his ears.

Outside, the place did change. The grass grew knee-high and spinach-thick. Shrubs burgeoned unchecked until they surrounded the little bungalow like a company of shaggy monsters. Even more troubling to Cleave Springs' second wave of settlers was the dead honey locust that stood in the side yard. Once in a while Hubbard would wander out to smoke beneath the branches of this upright corpse, succumbing to an attitude of desolate communion as he exhaled toward the stricken crown.

WHEN THE LETTER FROM THE CITIZENS' GROUP arrived Hubbard snickered darkly over its chummy threats and dropped it in the trash. The city followed with a letter of its own, promising to fine Hubbard if he didn't take action in his yard.

Resistance stirred in the disc jockey's breast. As summer settled in, he began to spend more time outside, standing defiantly under his dead honey locust, headphones on, cigarette dangling from his lips, while newcomers attached to strollers and leashes crossed the street to avoid passing too near him and his hazardous tree.

Hubbard took a grim kind of pleasure in his standoff with the neighborhood's swelling quaintness brigade. Life had always ambushed him in the past, attacking before he had a chance to shore up his position. Not this time. Never before had Hubbard been so prepared for a fight. His confidence bordered on outright smugness. If need be, he knew, he could hold his ground until a heap of bug-chewed pulp was all that remained of the honey locust.

"Let it rot," he would say aloud, standing at the kitchen sink as he peered through the window at his tree. "Let the fucker rot."

But one Friday afternoon, as headphoned Hubbard stood outside basking in his reader's voice, a ratty old pickup stopped at the curb. A man got out and approached the waist-high fence. He pointed toward the dead tree and warned Hubbard that if it didn't come down soon, one of its heavy branches would surely crush his roof.

"Is that the kind of damage you want?"

Hubbard pressed the pause button and dropped his cigarette in the rank grass.

"Why don't I come out here tomorrow mornin and take that thing down for you?" the man continued. "Get it out the way."

Hubbard accused the man of working for the city.

The man pointed back in the direction of his wretched truck. "Tell me somethin: does that look like part of the city's fleet?"

Hubbard asked him if he had a card.

The man scowled. "I'm standin right here lookin at you, man. What do I need a card for?"

Hubbard liked the tree man's answers. Also, he liked his look. His skin was the color of pecan meat, his hair was natty, his eyes were a stunning shade of green. Scar tissue from a burn swirled up one side of his neck and puckered the lower half of the ear. His shoulders were thick and his belly impressive. He told Hubbard to call him Junior. Hubbard guessed Junior was a few years shy of his own age: forty, maybe forty-two—well into the middle of his march.

Junior showed up early the next morning with two younger men, his nephews. Hubbard spent most of the day in his kitchen watching Junior and the nephews dismantle the tree. Junior wielded the chainsaw like a flyswatter. He hauled on ropes and barked orders and gestured to the young men with his powerful arms. Hubbard never considered leaving the house to avoid being hammered by a falling limb.

At the end of the day only the trunk remained, about house-high still, its thicker branches reduced to firewood and stacked alongside the fence while the thinner scraps lay heaped in the truck-bed. When Hubbard came outside he found Junior and the nephews standing in the driveway near the truck. Hubbard accepted the beer they offered and smiled bashfully as Junior ribbed his crew.

Junior said he would finish up the next morning and asked if he could store his tools in Hubbard's garage. Hubbard surprised himself by saying yes.

JUNIOR CAME ALONE Sunday morning. Watching through the kitchen window, Hubbard saw that several smartly dressed members of the Mt. Zion congregation stopped to chat with the tree man as they made their way to the church. Junior worked steadily, but the chainsaw quieted for a while when the gospel started to heat up, and he worked more fitfully then. He would pause to hear the last few bars of a song before yanking his saw to life. He nodded with satisfaction from time to time.

Hubbard's windows stood open to the music. He enjoyed watching Junior listen. The singers' sorrowful, impassioned voices spoke to Hubbard also, as did the lyrics of the songs.

> *Nobody knows the trouble I've seen*
> *Nobody knows but Jesus*
> *Nobody knows the trouble I've seen*
> *Glory hallelujah*

Hubbard had no ties to Jesus or any other deity. As he stood there swaying, borne along by the surging rhythms, he caught himself wishing he could know a god in the way these singers knew theirs.

The musical experience hardly seemed to slow Junior's work. Hubbard was dismayed by how rapidly the tree man rendered the mighty trunk into a heap of harmless sticks. He enjoyed having Junior on the premises.

Hubbard's mood was regretful as he descended the back porch stairs, checkbook in hand. He walked from the back yard around the corner of the house, pulling up when he caught sight of Junior standing in the front yard, feet wide apart, arms folded over belly, talking across the low fence to a large woman in a skirt and blazer the color of ripe tangerines. Worshippers streamed from the doors of the church, some lingering to chat in clots of three or four, others climbing into their cars. Hubbard was too far away to hear what Junior was saying, but he could see it made the woman smile. The sight of Junior standing there, proprietary, at ease, made Hubbard feel like a trespasser on his own property.

He went back the way he had come and sat down on the steps of his back porch. He gazed across toward the big brick store building, recently purchased by an artist-couple. The old shopkeeper, dour Mr. Keeler, had died nearly two years before of a massive stroke. Mrs. Keeler had hung on for a while before closing up shop and fattening her slot machine fund with the sale of the building. The artists lived upstairs and had converted the store space into studios. They had ripped the asphalt from much of the parking area and enlarged the back yard, where they used part of the space to grow vegetables. A tall wooden fence blocked Hubbard's view of the yard, but he could hear the artist-father in the garden with his small daughter.

"Hi little hair looms," the child sang. "Little hard greeny greens."

"*Heir* loom," the father corrected, "like air you breathe. Heirloom. It's a thing that's been in a family a long time. The old ones hand it down to the young ones."

"Someone old gave us these greenies?"

"In a way, yes. But you wait. They'll be red and soft pretty soon. Tasty, too."

A brief flash of white registered in Hubbard's peripheral vision and he looked up toward the building's second-story entrance, where the child's mother sat at the top of the fire escape with a drawing pad. The woman's face and her black hair were all Hubbard could see above the top of the large pad. She looked intently down at her mate and child in the garden, then back at her paper, then down again. She hadn't noticed Hubbard.

Junior wore a sour look on his face when he returned from the front of the house. "What's goin on with this here yard?"

Hubbard studied his own feet.

"I could look after it for you, man. Get it in shape and keep it that way, all season long."

"What would that cost me?"

"My sister, over here on Kramer Street, she's been lettin me keep stuff in the shed out back of her place. Now she's fixin to make her pile of money and move on."

"Her too, eh?"

"I heard that," Junior said. "Just saw big Nola coming out of Mt. Zion. She and I went to school together right up the street. She lives over in Prince George's now, comes to Cleave Springs for church on Sundays. Like half of them people."

"How about you?"

"Well I *been* living with my sister. I get that old place to where it's lookin right, next thing I know it's for sale and she's sayin I should come with her to North Carolina."

"You're not leaving?"

Junior scowled. "I left once before, joined the army. You know where that got me? Persian damn Gulf." He laughed ruefully, shaking his head.

Hubbard's eyes flitted toward the scar tissue on Junior's neck and ear.

"Made it back in one piece, mostly, and I ain't *leavin* again. This is where I'm *from*."

Junior turned toward the open garage door. "Tell you what. Rearrange things in here a little bit, looks like there'd be plenty of extra space."

Hubbard couldn't begin to think of what was stored in the small metal building.

"A trade?" he said.

"That's right. I get someplace to keep my things, you don't have this grass growin up here under your elbows."

JUNIOR WAS WAITING for Hubbard when he got home from work a couple of days later. Ladders, ropes, and tools filled the back of the truck.

Hubbard unlocked the garage door and Junior lifted it, saying he would pull everything out first and then figure out the best way to put it back in. Feeling faint, Hubbard took a step back and sat down awkwardly on the low brick wall that ran along the driveway.

Junior hurried over and knelt beside him.

Hubbard said he was fine but they agreed he should probably sit there for a few minutes. Junior took his house keys and brought him a glass of water from the kitchen. Then he began to empty the garage. When he had everything out, he stood on the driveway looking over the assortment of neglected belongings.

Eventually he raised one of his heavy arms and pointed at the baby furniture, the wooden high chair and crib, the cute old kid's chest of drawers. "That what made your knees weak?"

Hubbard didn't deny it.

"I'm listenin," Junior said, and sat down beside him on the brick wall.

That was all the prompting Hubbard needed. He spilled the whole bleak story of his time in the bungalow. It relieved him tremendously to share that information, to explain the baby furniture, to take the tree man in the house and show him what Leona had left behind. He led Junior into the bedroom so he could see the clothes in her closet and drawers. He lifted the lid on the jewelry box and let Junior peer inside. While they stood near the open box, Hubbard gushed to Junior about the first chapter of *Middlemarch*, when the two sisters, gentle young women, sort through and divide up the jewelry in the box their deceased mother has left behind. Junior listened to it all.

At the end of the evening, in a fever of gratitude, Hubbard rummaged through kitchen drawers until he found a spare key to the garage. He bestowed the key upon Junior with a gesture that was strangely ceremonial and antique, like a long-ago mayor standing at the gates of a small city, welcoming back one of its best and brightest sons.

❖ ❖ ❖

JUNIOR COMMENCED HIS ATTACK on Hubbard's yard by barbering the shrubs. Next he cut the lawn to carpet length and edged aggressively along the walks, creating what looked to Hubbard like a moat around the property. He trimmed dead limbs from the trees and put circular mounds of mulch around all their bases. He drew up a list of annuals, gave Hubbard the truck keys, and sent the disc jockey off to the nursery. With hoe and shovel, Junior reclaimed old flowerbeds at the base of the house and along its walkways.

He would come in the late afternoon and work in the yard for a couple of hours, then unload the belongings he had ferried over from his sister's place. The garage absorbed his first two loads without any trouble. The third one involved some head scratching. In the end, he had to carry a few items back behind the garage and store them under a tarp.

"You know what?" he said to Hubbard after he had stowed the entire fourth truckload under the same tarp. "It's about time for a sale." The summer evening was warm and Junior's shirt was soaked from his exertions.

"A sale," Hubbard said, lifting the lid on the grill so he could eye their burgers. The grill and lawn chairs were out of the garage for the first time in years.

"Got too much stuff anyway," Junior said, accepting a cold beer from Hubbard. "Who knows, I might earn enough to cover first and last month's rent somewhere." He laughed. "But I might not, either. Damn, Hubbard, you know what it cost to rent in Cleave Springs now?"

Junior left the yard and strolled the length of the driveway. "Yes sir," he said when he returned. "This driveway is a fine place for a sale. We could do it together. You got anything you're ready to part with?"

Hubbard lifted the lid off his grill again.

"I don't know," Junior said, "maybe it's still too soon."

The burger flipper clattered on the grill shelf before falling to the grass. "Just have your fucking sale, all right?" Hubbard turned and walked up the back porch steps.

Junior followed him into the kitchen. "Hold on, Hubbard. That was just an idea, man. If you don't like it, forget about it. You're the boss."

Hubbard didn't feel like the boss. Ten days before, in a moment of weakness, he had sat there next to the driveway with Junior and exposed himself utterly. If Junior looked to lord it over him and his property now, how could Hubbard blame him? Not that Hubbard *wanted* to blame him. The fact was Hubbard felt hopelessly fond of Junior. He had endured three solitary years. Now, he'd begun looking each evening for Junior to come. Whenever the tree man did appear, Hubbard invited him to stay for grilled meat and beer.

"Don't worry," Junior assured him. "Ain't nobody havin any sale."

"Have your sale!" Hubbard shouted. "Have it!" He put his face in his hands and wept.

Junior's large hand rested on his shoulder. "Poor Hubbard. You're mournin too."

❖ ❖ ❖

JUNIOR WAS RIGHT: Hubbard supposed he *was* mourning. Who knew that mourning would be such a messy affair? And painful. It didn't feel good at all. To Hubbard, this made it seem more necessary. But he had to wonder: what about those three years before Junior had barged into his world and lowered that burly shoulder against the stuck-shut door that guarded his emotions? If not mourning, what had Hubbard been doing all that time?

He resolved to go through with the sale. Since Junior had experience staging sales, he would run the show. The baby furniture would sell at a price Junior set or would go to the highest bidder. Junior advised Hubbard against selling Leona's clothing and shoes; with Hubbard's consent, the tree man bagged those items up and disposed of them through proper channels.

About the jewelry box Hubbard was undecided. He spent a weepy evening going through it alone at the kitchen table. A many-sectioned tray where Leona had stored the pieces she wore often fit above a deeper compartment below. In the lower part, Hubbard found necklaces and bracelets and earrings he had given her as gifts during their early years together, before it dawned on him that he had no clue what she actually liked. They had laughed about it at the time. Leona had been a woman of discernment; what had attracted her to Hubbard now struck him as a profound mystery, though he figured he had known once.

Hubbard slept even more poorly than usual the night before the sale. On a visit to the kitchen, around one o'clock, he saw through the window that Junior's truck was parked in his driveway. The sleeping tree man's bare foot was propped on the back of the seat. That sight disturbed Hubbard such that he couldn't even concentrate on his book. He shut off the player and lay blinking in the darkness. The sun was coming up by the time he began to doze.

WHEN HE AWOKE it was midmorning, bright and warm. He hurried to the kitchen, looked out, and saw that Junior had filled the driveway with items for sale. Now Junior was busy chatting with members of the Mt. Zion congregation as they made their way toward the church.

The service had started by the time Hubbard emerged to join Junior on the driveway. The church windows stood open. Mt. Zion's preacher ranted for a while, then the choir began to sing in a slow, stately cadence:

I shall not, I shall not be moved
I shall not, I shall not be moved
Just like a tree planted by the water
I shall not be moved

Business was steady throughout the morning, and the choir warmed to its task, building up the energy until it pumped out great swells of heart-shaking music. Hubbard stewed in a strong broth of feelings as passers-by perused the goods. A pregnant couple with an arthritic old beagle bought the baby furniture without even negotiating the price. A man purchased Junior's free weights for his teenage son. As agreed, Hubbard remained in the shadows while Junior handled the customers. Junior hustled the items arrayed on the driveway while also using Hubbard's made-over yard as a showroom to display his gardening skills.

"Haulin, tree removal, lawn care, I do all of that. You ever want me," Junior would say, gesturing toward Hubbard, "just talk to this man back over here. That's my agent."

The atmosphere livened up when the Mt. Zion service ended. Most of the congregation members stopped to examine the items on sale, a paltry banquet of old tools, sports equipment, books, cookware, and electronic devices. Junior grew more animated with this familiar crowd, teasing, laughing, and reminiscing. He brought a few people over for Hubbard to meet. His sixth grade teacher, a feisty woman in her seventies. A bald cousin who appeared to be Junior's age. A woman Hubbard recognized as the one who sported the tangerine suit the day that Junior had finished cutting up the dead honey locust.

Over and over, Junior reminded these people from his past that his sister had sold out and declared that he had no intention of living anywhere but Cleave Springs. He would not be moved.

IT WAS MID-AFTERNOON and quite hot by the time the Mt. Zion crowd had cleared. Hubbard fetched two beers from the fridge and he and Junior sat on the brick wall next to the driveway, shaded by the artist-couple's back yard fence.

For quite a while no one came by, and then the artists themselves appeared in the driveway, their small daughter hiding behind her father's legs. Hubbard recognized the black-haired mother from the time he'd seen her drawing up on the fire escape. At close range, he saw her hair was threaded with gray.

Hubbard shook hands with the woman and her husband and stooped to wave at the child, who had her mother's dark hair and her father's bottle-blue eyes. He instantly forgot their names.

The woman set down the basket of tomatoes she carried. "These are from our garden."

"Heirlooms?" Hubbard asked.

"Indeed." The woman turned briefly toward Hubbard's back porch. "Your house. It's the Starlight, isn't it?"

"Indeed," Hubbard said. "Sears, Roebuck. 1927."

"Is it perfect inside, too?"

Junior scoffed loudly.

"Perfect?" Hubbard said.

"I've had my eye on this place ever since we first came to look at our building. I love these houses. Most of them get wrecked by these god-awful additions people put on them."

"Come take a look," Hubbard said, and the woman eagerly followed him toward the back door.

Hubbard got beers for everybody before catching up with her in the living room.

"The furniture," she said, "the fixtures, everything is right. Somebody knew what they were doing."

"My late wife," Hubbard volunteered. He removed the framed packing slip from the wall and handed it over. "This house was her baby."

WHEN HUBBARD AND THE WOMAN came outside they found Junior dumping fresh briquettes on the grill. The child had discovered a red rubber ball among the unsold treasures and was kicking it back and forth with her father on the grass.

The whole scene worked on Hubbard's grief-steeped feelings. Before the family could dissolve it, he invited them to stay for a barbecue. They agreed, asking what they could contribute, and Hubbard reminded them about the tomatoes. Still, he accepted the woman's offer to make a potato salad, only because he liked the idea of her cooking something in his kitchen. She went back over to her place to get what she needed and Hubbard chatted with her husband about all the work they'd done on the old store building.

Before long the man asked Hubbard if they'd met somewhere before. "There's something so familiar about you…"

"*Demon here*," Hubbard said, "*rockin you through the lunch hour.*"

The man's eyes sprang open. "You're Demon? No way. I used to listen to you all the time. The Blue Plate Special, right? You still doing that?"

Hubbard belched loudly, then turned away, too shocked to excuse himself.

When the woman returned, the child joined her in the kitchen and the man helped Junior and Hubbard clear the driveway.

Later, while the burgers sizzled on the grill, Junior handed Hubbard some folded-up bills. "Most of that's for the baby furniture."

"How'd *you* do?"

Junior shook his head. "Bright side? All of what's left fits in the garage."

Hubbard pulled the burgers from the grill and carried them into the kitchen, where the air was hot from the boiling water. The woman had made a big bowl of potato salad and cooked the corn from Hubbard's fridge; the man had sliced up the tomatoes and tossed them with olive oil and basil leaves from his garden.

The child lifted her blue eyes up to Hubbard and asked if he had a jar.

"For fireflies," her mother explained. "I just saw one out the window."

While the others filled their plates Hubbard found a mayonnaise jar and used an ice pick to poke air holes in the lid. He descended the steps and handed the jar to the little girl. She pranced away while Junior shook his head.

"Should've seen this place when *I* was a boy. Thick with lightnin bugs back then. More crickets, too."

"You grew up here?" the woman said.

"Born and raised."

"You've seen a lot of changes."

"That's no lie."

"Honey, that reminds me," the woman said, putting her hand on the man's arm. "This house is the Starlight, like we thought. Dale has the packing slip from when all the pieces arrived in the railyard. 1927."

"Can I show him?" she said to Hubbard, rising from her lawn chair.

When she returned, her mate studied the framed document reverently in the failing light and then handed it to Junior. Junior glanced at it, rose, and dropped the frame in Hubbard's lap as he set off walking to the garage. He raised the metal door and disappeared inside for a while.

He returned to the yard with a shoe box and began to flip through its contents. "Here's a little more history for you," he said, handing an aged color photograph to the woman.

She examined the picture closely before handing it to Hubbard. "Your house, Dale."

Hubbard recognized his back porch instantly. He didn't know the people standing on the porch steps—a man, a woman, and four children, all of them dressed in what looked like Sunday clothes.

"Which one are you?" the woman said.

Junior rose and pointed to himself, the older of the two boys.

"Wait a minute," the man said. "You grew up in this house?"

Junior straightened his back and closed his eyes. "My daddy, Fulton Chalmers, bought it from Mr. Franklin Peters, the name on that packing slip, in 1961."

"And the people I bought it from?" Hubbard said.

Now Junior's eyes were wide open. "My sisters, my brother, they sold it right after Mama died. Didn't figure they'd wait for me to get back from the battlefield. Didn't figure I might want to hang onto the place, soldier might want a home to come back to. Person they sold it to kept it for a few years, probably got tired of waitin for the neighborhood to turn around. Then you bought it."

"Imagine," the woman said. "And now here the two of you are—friends."

Friends. The word settled upon the two men like dust on a fresh set of fingerprints. They stayed quiet for a quarter of an hour, watching and listening as the parents started preparing their child to go back home. The kid had lost interest in the fireflies before she'd managed to catch any; the jar lay near the foot of her mother's chair. Hubbard picked it up and took it inside with his plate and a couple of beer bottles. Soon everyone but Junior was busy cleaning up. Hubbard enjoyed the bustle in his kitchen; he even liked the sounds coming from the whining child, who sensed that bedtime was drawing near.

He went into the unused bedroom and retrieved Leona's jewelry box from the top of the dresser. Back in the kitchen he called the little girl over, set the box on the tabletop and opened the lid, telling her to choose something. The whining stopped. The child's deep blue eyes gazed upon Leona's jewelry as if it were a priceless trove. She looked up at her mother, who nodded encouragement. Then with surprising deftness the child reached in and plucked out a bracelet, several turquoise stones set in linked pieces of silver.

"I'm no good with names," Hubbard said to the child. "Tell me yours again."

"Claire."

"And your mommy's and daddy's names?"

"Eleanor and George."

"Claire, that bracelet used to belong to a woman named Leona. She would say you made a good choice."

When his neighbors were gone Hubbard peered out the window and made sure that Junior was still in his chair. He carried the jewelry box back to the bedroom and placed it on the dresser. Then he opened the dresser's empty top drawer, walked across the hall to the other bedroom, and removed a stack of underwear from the closet where he kept his clothes. He brought them back and stowed them in the dresser drawer. He transferred the rest of his clothes from the closet to the dresser and then put clean sheets on the double bed that he was going to have to learn to sleep on again. He put fresh sheets on the futon in the other room as well. All the while, he sang quietly to himself:

> *Claire, Eleanor, and George*
> *Claire, Eleanor, and George*
> *George and Claire and El-ea-nor*
> *Claire, Eleanor, and George*

On the way back outside he stopped at the fridge to get a couple of beers. He lingered a moment in front of the sink, peering through the window into his side yard, all that open space where the dead tree had stood—would still be standing if Junior hadn't come along.

After a few minutes he went outside and sat down. He rested a hand on his friend's shoulder. "Fulton Chalmers, Junior," he said. "You're home."

LILY PAD

Yreka

Journal, he came in today, and he wasn't alone.

Ricky saw him first. "What did that boy take out of his backpack?"

I was steaming milk for a latte and I didn't look up right away because I knew Ricky was watching me. I kept my eyes down on my work until that latte was full of froth. I handed it over to the customer and gave her a warm Lily Pad smile. And then I looked over. Tre was already inside, sitting down at the table he likes near the ice water, and there was a sack sitting on the chair across from him.

"What is it?" Ricky said.

It looked like a sack of flour in little purple overalls, but I didn't say that to Ricky. "Beats me."

Pretty soon Tre stood up and started walking over.

"Look at the way that boy walks," Ricky whispered. "Drags his feet. Slumps his shoulders. How can he see through those bangs?"

Ricky has excellent posture. Trims that black hair every week. Always looks nice. Smells nice, too.

"Hi there," Ricky said.

Tre nodded. "Ricky. What's up? How's it going, Yreka?"

"It's going," I said. "Can I get you something?"

Tre takes forever to decide, which is strange because he always orders the same thing—Red Bull. It's in the refrigerator case, self-service, so there's nothing I can do for him except ring it up. He was patting out a rhythm on his thighs, standing across from the counter, looking around, or trying to see through his bangs. Eventually he walked over to the case and got his Red Bull. He brought it to the register.

I asked if that was a sack of flour sitting at the table with him.

"It is."

"What's it doing there?"

"It's, like, a school project. Ten pounds, seven days." He shrugged. "I don't know. They want us to see what it's like to be, like, depended on. By a baby or whatever."

"What school do you go to?"

"Saint Bernard."

"Saint Bernard," I said. "Who was that?"

"I think it's, like, a really big dog?"

He turned around and walked back to his table.

"Damn, Y," Ricky whispered, "how can somebody so dumb be so damn sexy?"

Tre

so mister curley this is my 1st letter. remember you said i could write letters to you because i dont do journaling and never have and you want us to journal about our flower sacks?

so day 1 with my flower sack was pretty cool. i decided to name the kid glen after glen dankley the guitarist for head cheese and im listening to head cheese right now what a noisy noisy band but strangely the noise helps me think. dont be fooled by the name glen mister curley because my flower sack kid is really a girl.

on the way home from school i walked into the bumble bee this store on the avenue with all kinds of baby clothes in it and i bought glen a little outfit a 1 piece thingy that was kind of purple not exactly a boy color or a girl color. the lady helped me put it on her rite in the store.

then i stopped at the lily pad for a red bull i needed some energy and glen sat in there on her own chair which is different from a real baby which wood have to sit on my lap or in 1 of those little car seats that come rite out of the car and sit on the floor of a place like the lily pad. is that cheating?

and then i walked down to the music shop and did my shift and it was really slow almost nobody came in just some kids for there lessons with jack my boss. its not that hard of a job. i had to apply for it and everything but i already new jack from taking lessons and i think maybe him and my mom set the hole thing up to pump up my self esteem. glen sat up on the counter next to the register. jack is cool with me playing 1 of the guitars when no customers need help so i took down this sweet gibson and played a few cords of the new one for little glen. i like to listen to hard noisy tunes but the ones that come out of me are peaceful.

after work i came home and ate dinner and introduced my mom to little glen. she said a baby wow that sounds like such a cool project and she was smiling hard as she said it.

and then she pulled out my biology book and started helping me study for the quiz tomorrow. i learn best threw my ears so she was reading to me about what the mitocondria do and you know what mister curley i really dont care what they do or if i get a bad grade for not knowing. so i listened for a minute but then i stuck my earbuds in and turned on some head cheese. she reached over and pulled the buds out so then i put my fingers in my ears and she started to give me a talking to which i couldnt here too well and then she slapped the table with both hands and walked away.

i put my earbuds back in and listened to a little more head cheese waiting for my dad to get home from work. when he walked in i shut off the music and introduced him to little glen and he asked why the hell i was carrying around a sack of flower in purple overalls and i told him all about the project.

this is for school he said.

it is.

saint bernard he said shaking his head. this is what im paying all that money for?

he went downstairs to his wine cellar and then i came up to my bedroom and pulled out my laptop to write this letter all about my day with glen finally some homework i can do and i dont just open it up and feel all shitty. mister curley is it a problem if i write shitty sense this is informal writing and shitty is how doing homework makes me feel? or not doing it as the case may be.

Yreka

Journal, I looked up Saint Bernard. He was a monk, born in the year 923. They made him a saint because he helped Catholic pilgrims walking across high mountain passes in the Alps on their way from France and Germany to Rome. He didn't do it all by himself. He created these hostels, which other monks helped him run, and kept running after he died in 1008. These monks would take care of the pilgrims and help them if they had trouble with snowstorms or avalanches. The dogs that helped the monks were the local herding dogs of that region; they came to be known as Saint Bernards.

Hostel: 1) A supervised, inexpensive lodging place for travelers; 2) an inn; a hotel.

Hostile: 1) Of, relating to, or characteristic of an enemy; 2) feeling or showing enmity or ill will, antagonistic; 3) unfavorable to health or well-being; inhospitable or adverse.

Maybe I'll bring up *hostel* and *hostile* tomorrow in AP English. Mrs. Naylor would swoon. She says I show great sensitivity to language, but I'd have to be asleep to miss the connection between this pair of homophones.

Granny and Arthur are in the kitchen right now, one thin wall between us, and she's feeding him dinner with angry talk for sauce.

"Where you been today?"

"Out workin," he says. "Detailed two cars roof to tires, cut the grass at four different houses."

"You been out drinkin, that's where you been."

"Had a beer after I finished, quench my thirst. Ain't nothin wrong with that."

"They is if you want to stay in <u>this</u> house. I won't have it. I got too much invested in that child. Too much blood, too much sweat, too <u>damn</u> many tears."

Tre

so mister curley im writing this letter at the lily pad. a lot of people that are buying and fixing up crappy old houses nearby are having babies and they like to bring them into the lily pad so its kind of cool to bring glen in here. back when my parents moved hear the neighborhood was all trashed not a lot of people were starting families in cleave springs and so there arent that many kids my age that live on the blocks around me. but people my age work in the lily pad like yreka and ricky. there both cool.

rite after school they dont have a lot of business so we talk sometimes. yreka just came over and i invited her to come and here me at the open mic night this coming sunday and she said she wood try to be there and then she told me who saint bernard was. i thought the school was named after the dogs but she said the dogs were actually named after the guy who was a monk in the alps who helped people get threw the snow. yreka told me that her and rickys school is named after timothy grimes who was a racist that wanted black kids and white kids to have separate schools forever. i said my dad went to grimes too back in the day and ricky said they dont need flower sacks at grimes because they have plenty of real babies.

yreka told me she liked my little flower sacks outfit and asked if it has a name and i told her glen is the name but its a girl. i also told her that from now on glen wont be sitting on chairs by herself witch is something real babies cant do. im way into this assignment mister curley and im going to treat glen like a real baby as much as possible. she was sitting on my lap wile i talked to yreka.

names are interesting according to yreka. she asked why im called tre and i said tre means three in italian and my real name is joseph salvatore verdi the third. my grandpa is called joseph my dad is sal and calling me tre is supposed to make everything simple and easy.

yreka went back behind the counter because some customers came in and i wrote most of my letter and then decided to carry glen over there and tell her one last thing before i left. this is what i wanted to say—yreka you have a most excellent name.

but there was a mini rush of customers all of a sudden and the line got kind of long and i sat hear and watched her for a minute and i noticed this little gold pin she was wearing on her shirt witch gave me an idea for my song. i didnt want to mess up her focus so i just rapt glen up in her blanket and left.

Yreka

Journal, there was a little lull this afternoon while he was drinking his Red Bull, so I decided it would be a good time to refill the ice water pitchers. We got to talk for a few minutes before Ricky butted in. Ricky gets under my skin sometimes. He acts like he's so in love with Tre, but then he says Tre is dumb.

Today Tre was holding the flour sack baby on his lap while

we talked. Glen, he calls it. He opened up the zipper on Glen's little outfit and showed me how he taped an index card to her belly with contact information on it.

GLEN VERDI
PLEES RETURN ME TO 303 SPRING STREET IF
YOU FIND ME
YOU WILL GET A REWARD

"I don't think I'd ever, like, lose her," he said. "But I do have kind of a history of losing things." He mentioned all the pairs of gloves he's lost, the winter coats, ski poles, swimming goggles, a scooter, a pair of skates, and a guitar.

"People do lose kids," he said. "It's on the news."

Granny is so scared of losing me that she tries to control every last thing I do. 16 years old, and I'm still getting directions from her on what streets to walk between home and work. Usually I follow her orders, but today I went a few blocks out of my way so I could walk past 303 Spring, a red brick two-story with a flag fluttering over the porch steps, not an American flag but a purple flag with pink and red hearts on stems gathered up tight like a bouquet. I stayed on the opposite side of the street as I passed, and I didn't slow down. Tre lives four blocks away from me, in another world. I can actually remember the days when Spring Street was part of my world. When I was little Granny used to take me to Mr. and Mrs. Keeler's store, right next door to Tre's house, for lollipops. Mr. Keeler died a few years ago. The store closed down and some white people bought the building to renovate. Mrs. Keeler moved in with her daughter, and Granny says she's spending all the money she got for the building at casinos.

I paused at the corner to take one last look back at Tre's house, and when I turned to head home there was Arthur standing in the middle of the sidewalk in front of me. Arthur and his shopping cart full of tools. Arthur and his wild, matted hair. Arthur and his hollow cheeks, his dirty shirt, his pants that barely clung to his scrawny waist.

"Ain't this a nice surprise," he said. "What brings you this way?"

"Walking home from work."

"Takin a detour?"

"Maybe."

He smiled. "Your detour got a name?"

"Is that your business?"

He shook his head. "Naw. Yards and cars—that's my business."

"You're working hard today, it looks like."

"Every day, girl. Every day. Got a lot of makin up to do, don't I?"

The next thing I knew Arthur was coming around from behind his cart, approaching me with the same hot look Granny gets in her eyes. He pointed. "What's that?"

"What, my pin?"

"That's right. What kinda pin is that?"

"It's for this club I'm in. I just got it yesterday."

"You in a club?"

"It's called the National Honor Society."

"The National Honor Society," he repeated in a hushed voice. "Because you so smart?"

"I do okay in school."

Arthur looks nothing like the fresh-faced kid in the pictures on the living room wall, but he still has a quality smile.

"Yreka," he said, "that's something to be proud of."

He stepped forward and began to spread his arms, like he wanted to hug me, but my hand shot out and he moved back, reaching to shake. The smile wilted fast.

Tre

so mister curley before dinner i was out on the front porch swing with my guitar and little glen was napping on her blanket and i was playing cords feeling my way threw this new song. arthur the guy who takes care of our cars was down on the driveway washing and detailing my moms mercedes and my dads expedition.

but suddenly he was on the porch saying he herd somebody up hear making music. turns out he is a musician too or used to be and he played trumpet. in fact he played with my dad in the grimes high school marching band and my dad played a horn too a sax witch i never new before.

sal verdi arthur said and he leaned his head over toward the cars down on the driveway and said old sal verdis not fixing phone lines anymore.

hes way up there in management now i said but im not sure arthur herd me because he had gotten all interested in glen. he wanted to know what was going on with the little bundle on the porch floor so i explained to him all about the flower sack assignment and he got kind of serious with me and came over close to me and told me children are the most important thing there is and whatever i do i should never never never let anybody take my child away. it was kind of intense.

my dad came out of the house and he was surprised to see arthur sitting on the swing next to me. my dad is touchy about lines. he built this little wine cellar in the basement and theres like this force field around that room and if you cross over the line wile hes in there smoking his cigar and drinking his wine he looks at you like your a burglar invading his property. he kind of looked like that at arthur even though he was hiring arthur to wash and detail the cars and the job was finished and arthur and me were just sitting there on the porch swing wile little glen napped.

i invited arthur to come to open mic at the lily pad this sunday then my dad and arthur walked down off the porch together so my dad could inspect the job and pay him. when my dad came back up i told him i never new he played sax and went to high school with arthur.

that was a long time ago he said. arthur was a couple years behind me.

were you and arthur serious about music i asked him.

i dont know he said. arthur wanted me to be in his quartet.

arthur had a quartet? cool. did you play in it?

i had just graduated he said. my dad had a job lined up for me with the phone company. i had real work to do.

music isnt real work?

could of been for arthur he said. he had talent. could of gone places.

i asked why he didn't and my dad said he remembered it having to do with a girl who got pregnant and arthur was the father and then he got into some other bad stuff.

i enjoy being a father i said.

he looked at me like i was a werewolf or something so i smiled and pointed down at little glen.

oh you mean the flower sack he said. god damn tre you scared the shit out of me. do me a favor. if your going to monkey around with girls make sure you got a condom handy.

at school they say we should practice abstinence.

well isnt that nice. do me a favor and get yourself some condoms in case abstinence doesnt work out.

what other bad stuff did arthur get into i asked.

its not important he said. the guys messed up but its not like he wood ever do violence to anybody. he came back a few months ago and weve been hiring him to do the cars. im glad to help him but you listen to me. you dont know the first thing about dealing with people like arthur. let me deal with him from now on. you keep clear.

i did violence to somebody i said.

i guess you did he said.

fyi mister curley i dont know what the school told you about the kid i beat up last year but i want to tell you myself that i didnt just attack him. he mocked the way i do rhythms on my thighs and the way i bob my head sometimes and he called me dumbass and shit for brains and stuff like that. but only when he shoved me did i start to pound him.

Yreka

Journal, I decided to quit wearing the pin. I put it back in the little velvet box and placed the box on top of my dresser. As soon as Granny sat down at the supper table this evening she noticed I wasn't wearing it and asked why. I told her it attracts too much attention.

"What kind of attention?"

"I bumped into Arthur on my way home and he got all excited about it," I said. "Tried to hug me."

Granny shook her head. "Didn't do a lick of the work, but wants the credit. Ain't that the way."

"They teased me about it this morning," I said.

"Who did?"

"Girls at the bus stop kept asking what the pin was for. Wouldn't leave it alone. I told them about the National Honor Society. One of them said, 'Is that a club for bitches who think they better?'"

Granny's eyes were full of fight. "Who said that? Did Chante say that? She'll be sorry she did when I tell her mama."

"It's not important who said it, Granny."

"Tamika? Reese? Me and their granny go all the way back. Was it one of them?"

She waited a minute for me to answer, and then she scowled.

"Yreka, you keep away from them girls, you hear me? You wait for that bus on the other side of the street."

"Don't worry, Granny. They don't want me getting near them."

"Good. That's what your granny want to hear."

"But Granny," I said, "someday, somebody might want to be near me."

She shook her head solemnly. "Have to get by me first."

"But what if I want to get near them, too?"

"Sound like you got somebody in mind." She planted her elbows on the table and rested her chin on her fists. "Who is it?"

I looked at my lap.

"Might as well tell me, child, before I find out. Your granny know everybody in this neighborhood."

"Everybody?" I said.

"Girl, what you tryin to do, rile me up? We got rules in this house."

"You can't protect me forever, Granny. Shouldn't I be learning how to take care of myself?"

"In time, child, in time."

"But I'm not a child."

Her laugh was cold. "You ain't no woman, neither."

Tre

so mister curley my mom said she thinks this is a cool project but guess what? usually shes great about helping with my homework she cares about it way more than i do but i just cant get her to help with glen at all. as you know im trying to go for total and absolute 100% reality with this flower sack baby and that means i need some help from time to time like today i wanted to take a shower and i asked my mom if she could hold glen on her lap for like 20 minutes. she said maybe it was time for glen to take a nap.

no i said glen just woke up from a nap a half hour ago and no way is she ready to go down again.

my mom said look tre its good that your taking this so seriously but i dont think there wood be anything wrong with a little brake.

parents dont get brakes i said. they either do what they need to do when the baby is napping or they hire a baby sitter or they ask family for help. your family and im asking for your help rite now. can you do this?

tre she said did you just call your flower sack baby she?

did i?

is glen a boy or a girl?

i thought about lying to her but that seemed wrong. glen is really a baby girl i said.

she winced like i had pulled a bandaid off her really fast.

why do you ask i said.

just curious she said.

Yreka

Journal, I'm giddy. I stayed up pretty late finishing my history essay and then I went to the kitchen for a snack. I was standing at the counter, eating a piece of cherry pie, listening to Granny snore, when the need to be free of this house rose up in me like a strong gust. I went back to my room and put on my sweatshirt. A girl on Spring Street would have snuck out her bedroom window, but my window is all blocked up by a thick cage of rusty screen. I went back to the kitchen to make sure Granny was still snoring, peeked into the living room where Arthur was asleep on the couch, and then slipped out the front door into the night. Oh, delicious!

I flipped up the hood of my sweatshirt and started walking. I wasn't scared at all, just giddy, delighted. Bold. I walked for quite a while, not exactly wandering, because I knew my destination was 303 Spring. I just took my time getting there. I had no set plan. I just wanted to think about Tre's life outside the Lily Pad, look at the house where he sleeps.

I stayed on the opposite side of the street and stopped before I got to the front of the house. The purple flag with its bouquet of hearts swayed in the breeze. From the angle I had I could see along the side of the house to an upstairs window where the light was still on. Was that his room? Was he in there right now, sitting on his bed maybe, strumming his guitar, practicing his music for the open mic Sunday evening? Was he being really quiet so as not to wake little Glen? Where was she? In a bassinet on the floor? Maybe she was in bed, cuddled up in the crook of his arm.

When the front door opened I nearly crumpled to the ground. I should have run away but there was no moving me. The porch light was on and I could see her perfectly. I know her face from the Lily Pad. She comes in once in a while with a book and orders a medium dark roast, no room for cream. Sad eyes. Always alone. And alone now, out on the porch in the night. She stood there for a minute, tapped a cigarette out of the pack and lit it. Then she opened the front door again, reached in and turned off the porch light. It was dark up under the roof of the porch but I watched the cigarette ember to track her movements.

She went to the swing at the far end of the porch and sat. She was facing in my direction. With the streetlights above, it must have been easy for her to see me.

I couldn't just stand there like a prowler. I had to do something. The first thing I did was remove my hood. Still bold, I started walking, but not back the way I had come. I walked past the front of number 303, my eyes on the house the whole time, and I could tell by watching the ember that she was watching me.

Tre

so mister curley earlier today glen was lying on her blanket on my bedroom floor and i was sitting on my bed polishing a couple of ruff spots in the new song and my mom knocked and opened the door before i could answer it.

did someone strike gold she asked.

in a way i said.

thats a new song isnt it? i dont remember hearing you play it before.

yeah i said i want to try it out at open mic night.

she smiled. i love to here you working on your songs. music is your release isnt it? everybody needs to have that.

i asked what she has and she blinked her eyes a bunch of times and her face turned a little red but after a minute she said she guessed her release was reading. my escape anyway she said. it seemed like we were threw but she didnt walk away. what else i said.

theres a girl who works at the lily pad. pretty. slight. well spoken. a black girl. do you know her?

why do you ask?

i saw her walking past the night before last she said. she was looking at our house.

i glanced over the side of the bed down at glen on the floor. asleep i whispered and waved my mom out of the room.

Yreka

Journal, I should have gone home at the end of my shift. But Tre had mentioned more than once that open mic night was coming and it seemed like he hoped I'd be there. So I told Granny they were short on workers and I had to pull a double shift. I don't like lying to her, but I knew she'd never figure this one out because she'd no sooner set foot in the Lily Pad than she would on the North Pole. So Ricky and I finished our shift and then we went down to the taqueria for something to eat.

"So, Y," Ricky said, "Bangs is going to be on stage. You excited?"

"I am looking forward to hearing him play. I'm curious."

"You're more than curious."

My face got warm. "Why do you say that?"

He smiled. "Because, Y, I'm alive. I have eyes. I see what happens to you when he walks in the door."

"God, do you think he notices?"

"Honestly, I don't know what's going on behind those bangs. Except for one thing: he likes you."

"How can you tell?"

"Everybody else in the whole café could strip down naked and that boy would never even notice it. He'd be looking at you."

I just assumed Ricky was coming to open mic with me but

he said he was going home to get ready for a party in DC. I asked what kind of party and he said the less I knew about that, the better.

"What about school tomorrow?" I asked.

"I'll probably sleep through it. Do me a favor, though, will you?"

"What?"

"Don't tell your friends at the National Honor Society."

We said goodbye in front of the taqueria and then I went back to the Lily Pad. It was strange to be there as a customer, strange to be there for Tre instead of hoping to see him during my shift. Nikki made me a mocha that I didn't really want and I carried the warm cup through the arch into the deep room.

The room was about half full, and I walked along answering the look of every regular with my Lily Pad smile. Tre was already there. Glen sat on his knee and his guitar case sat on the floor next to his chair. He looked surprised to see me. "Nikki told me you were off," he said.

"I came to hear you play."

He stood up, clutching Glen against his hip. "Um, sit down?"

I sat in the chair next to his. He sat back down, looked away from me and started patting a rhythm out on his thighs.

I sat there beside him as the room filled up and Gordon the attorney, the master of ceremonies, welcomed everybody. The first musician, a college girl named Lindsey who drinks a lot of chai, started strumming her guitar and singing into the microphone and I didn't pay careful attention to her song, which seemed to be saying that life is like a used car lot. I was too busy wondering if I was on my first date. Here I was sitting next to

Tre, who had invited me to be here. True, he hadn't picked me up from home, he hadn't taken me anywhere. But this was the first time I'd made this kind of effort to spend time with him. I liked the way it felt.

The second musician was Fred the furniture maker who plays Scrabble with his friends on Tuesday afternoons. Fred played the accordion, not very well. When he finished, Gordon went to the microphone and announced that Tre was next. Tre stood up, holding Glen under one arm, and bent down for his guitar. He walked a few steps up toward the stage and then turned back toward me.

"Yreka, could you, like, hold Glen while I play?"

I took Glen and sat down with her on my knee while everybody everybody everybody looked at me. I stared straight ahead at the microphone, my face burning. The microphone was set up in the bay window next to the door, so I saw Arthur as soon as he came in. His hair was wild and matted but his shirt and pants were clean. He didn't notice me. But he noticed Tre's mother, who came in a few minutes later with a man whose hair told me what Tre's would look like if it ever got cut. He had to be Tre's father, Sal. They all shook hands and chatted near the door while Tre tuned up his guitar.

And then Tre stepped up to the microphone and said, "I'm Tre Verdi. I have two songs to play. This first one's called 'Cleave Springs'."

They were polite, this Lily Pad crowd. They'd been polite for Lindsey and at least tolerant while Fred strutted around with his accordion and flapped his arms like chicken wings. Tre's music made their manners unnecessary. Having the guitar in his hands, the microphone there to take his voice, the people there to listen—it just seemed to organize him. He was together. His sound came so cleanly to my ears. There were the chords he played, there was his voice, and the place where chords meshed with voice was as tender as a new bruise.

As soon as the song finished, Tre slumped back into his usual self, waiting for the applause to end.

"This next tune is, like, dedicated to someone who works here at the Lily Pad." He looked straight across the room to me and started to strum and sing. Again everyone's eyes were on me, but this time there weren't just the eyes of all the Lily Pad regulars, this time there were Arthur's eyes, Tre's mother's eyes, his father's eyes, all of them watching me as Tre sang to me, Yreka, the girl who makes the lattes and the small talk, the girl who smiles her Lily Pad smile, the girl from another world, the girl holding his baby, the girl in his song.

And when the song ended? I couldn't stay to find out.

Tre

so mister curley my new song is called yreka and i played it at the open mic and she was in the audience. i think she got to here the hole thing before she rapt up little glen and ran out into the street gone. just gone.

will letting somebody kidnap my flower sack baby trash my grade for this assignment? i know it looks bad and doesnt pump up my credentials as a father but the thing is mister curley number 1 i was stunned when it happened. we all were. everyone in

the room went quiet and forgot to clap for my song and number
2 i trusted yreka not to let anything happen to little glen. if i didnt
trust her wood i of asked her to hold glen wile i played?

when i finished people came at me saying how good the
music was but i pushed threw them out to the sidewalk trying to
see witch way yreka ran. my parents came up behind me and said
how great my songs were but i just wanted to know what happened to yreka and glen. my dad said not to worry because arthur
went after her and he wood catch up with her before long.

why did arthur go after her i said.

hes her father my dad said.

YREKA IS ARTHURS CHILD i yelled. WHY DIDN'T
YOU TELL ME THAT?

YOU DIDNT TELL ME YOU WERE IN HER PANTS
he yelled back.

i punched him in the face hard. he stumbled backward but
then got his feet set and stood looking at me with blood under
his nose and fists ready. i wood of kept pounding at him but my
hand felt broken. i sat down in one of the outdoor chairs and
started crying.

WHAT THE FUCK TRE my dad shouted. my mom tried
to quiet him down but when verdis get excited they dont like to
be shushed. he batted her hand away. WHATS YOUR FUCK-
ING PROBLEM SON?

yrekas gone i said. glen is gone.

he sat down next to me. you mean that sack of fucking
flower? i can buy you ten sacks of flower kid. its not like you lost
a real child.

i cried louder.

oh fuck my dad said grabbing his face with his hands. fuck fuck fuck. is that what this is about?

my mom kneeled down between us. tre told me glen is a girl baby she said.

why did you name it glen my dad said.

I WOOD OF NAMED IT AFTER MY SISTER IF I NEW HER FUCKING NAME.

my dad looked at my mom. i thought you told him about it he said.

at least she told me i had a sister i said. thats more than you did. she only told me because i found that little pacifier. i asked my sisters name and she didnt tell me.

why not my dad asked her.

my mom was crying too hard to answer him.

she refused i said. she told me to go ask you.

Yreka

Journal, I always loved going to the playground in the right of way on really cold days, days when it was so cold no other kids would venture out. Those times I had the big tube slide all to myself. I'd go in at the bottom and climb up halfway, then get sideways and wedge myself in there, snug in my coat, hat, and gloves—quiet, peaceful, invisible. It bothered Granny. She knew that's where I was, but she didn't like it. "Come on out of there, child. Come out where Granny can see you." I never got to stay as long as I would have liked.

The playground was deserted when I got there today. It

wasn't that cold, but the sun was getting low and all the little kids
were probably at home having dinner. I went straight to the slide.
I could actually still fit inside, but I'm too big now to curl up in
there comfortably. After trying it, I settled down at the bottom
of the slide with Glen on my lap and my feet on the ground. I
sat for an hour or more before Arthur arrived.

"I looked all over," he said, "and then it hit me."

"What did?"

"You was always wantin the slide."

"How would you know?"

"I brought you here all the time, girl."

"I only remember coming with Granny."

"This is way back when you was an itty bitty thing, just startin
to talk. 'Mommy Daddy slide. Mommy Daddy slide.'"

"I don't remember her."

"Well," he said, "she was pretty like you. Smart, too." He
glanced down at little Glen. "Just too damn young to raise you
up. That's what your granny decided."

"You thought different?"

He shook his head. "Hard woman, your granny. We was too
soft to fight her, too young to prove her wrong. When your
mama run off, I had my troubles, that just proved your granny
right. But I ain't too young no more. I'm back—"

"Don't say it," I said. "I don't want to hear that again."

We eyed each other a minute. Then I said, "Who named
me?"

"Your mama and me. We was so proud, you was such a beautiful baby, it was like Tre's song said—we struck gold."

"You should have consulted a dictionary," I said.

"We knew how to spell the word, but your mama, she liked the letter Y. Said it had two arms reaching up into the sky, celebrating. I never had looked at it that way."

"I hadn't either." The words came out softer than I intended. He leaned forward like he might try to hug me, but I shoved him back with new words. "You know Tre's parents."

"Sal Verdi," he nodded. "Grew up right over here on Spring. We went to Grimes together—he was a junior my freshman year. Played sax in the marching band."

"You were friends?"

He smiled. "Friends wasn't allowed. Friendly was. Me and Sal, we had things in common. Both liked jazz, both played horns. And then we both had baby girls we couldn't keep."

"Tre had a sister?"

He nodded again, sorrowful. "Still a baby when they lost her. Two, three months old? Sal ain't healed from that. I see it because I knew him before." He glanced at Glen again. "How well you know the boy?"

"Well, we've discussed names."

That shut him up. Neither of us said anything as we walked to Tre's house. We paused at the bottom of the porch steps under the hearts and Arthur offered to wait, but I told him not to. I climbed the steps, rang the doorbell and stepped back off the mat. To my right, a curtain moved, but I was too slow to see who had peeked through it. Pretty soon Tre opened the door.

He came out onto the porch and shut the door behind him. I offered Glen, but only his left hand reached out to take her. The right was heavily bandaged. I asked what happened.

"Cracked a couple of fingers," he said.

"How?"

"No big deal. Went to Urgent Care, barely had to wait." He flipped the bangs away from his eyes. "Um, Yreka, I'm so sorry. I should have, like, warned you."

"About what?"

"My song upset you. That was so not cool."

"I came to give an apology," I said. "Not to get one."

He shrugged.

"Glen's important to you. I never should have run off with her."

"Why did you?"

"She's yours."

"And you wanted to, like, take her?"

"To be her, I think."

He knelt to place Glen on the wicker couch. Upright again, he faced me, his left hand patting a rhythm out on his thigh.

I patted my thighs. "Why do you do it?"

"Calms me down," he said, and stopped patting. The calm left his body like smoke from a chimney.

"Listen, it's dark. Would you mind walking me home?"

"Oh," he said. "Great."

I reached the sidewalk first and turned back as he descended the steps. "What about Glen?"

"She's staying," he said.

He patted his left thigh while we walked, which kind of bothered me. At the first corner, I reached out and took hold of his hand.

"Okay," he said after a few steps. "Yeah."

We held hands until we got to my house, where we found

Arthur sitting outside on the sagging porch steps like a father waiting for his daughter to return from a date. The broken rain gutter hung in the air above him.

"Uh oh," Arthur said, pointing at Tre's wrapped hand. "Who'd you smack?"

"My dad," Tre said. "Broke two fingers."

Arthur's eyebrows lifted. "Smacked your daddy? Now, don't you be givin Yreka ideas."

"Too late," I said, and Arthur laughed.

"Just your strummin hand," he said, serious again. "That's lucky. Tell you what, Tre. You got somethin goin on with that music, my friend. You sound good."

Tre looked at me.

"Very good," I said.

He looked around, as if he wasn't sure how to get back to his house. I glanced up the sidewalk in the right direction and he turned that way.

"Tomorrow?" he said.

"I'm off tomorrow, but I'll be there Tuesday."

"Tuesday," he repeated, like he was memorizing a new word.

"Your granny went to bed early," Arthur said as we watched Tre walk away. "Not feelin too good. Frettin about your detour."

"How can you tell?"

"Sent me out a minute ago to get you from work, said she didn't want you walkin home in the dark. Wants the names of any boys I see doggin around that Lily Pad."

I told him I'd lied to Granny about pulling a double shift. "She never would have let me stay for the open mic."

He smiled. "That's between you and me."

"That too," I said.

"Yeah, that too."

Tre

mister curley sorry im handing in the last two letters a day late. my parents kept me out of school today so we could go on a little family trip and we drove out to a cemetery in maryland where all the verdis have there graves. i was there once before when my dads mother died and i was six or seven years old. when my sister died i was barely two and they decided not to take me out there for the funeral. her name was isabella and i really dont remember her but she was a healthy baby seven weeks old when my dad fell asleep on the couch with her on his chest one night and he rolled over and pinned her against the back pillows and when he woke up she wasnt breathing.

i asked my mom and dad why they never told me about my own sister and my mom said they were selfish and it hurt them to think about her so they just pretended like she never lived.

the thing is mister curley she kind of did live and i sensed it all along. and then one day when i was 12 i was searching around the house for this guitar pick i lost just searching anywhere and everywhere because i really needed that pick. the jewelry box on my moms dresser has these really shallow drawers just right for a flat little guitar pick and i thought who knows she could of found my pick and slipped it into one of them. I started sliding those drawers open and they were filled with earrings and necklaces and whatnot but in one of them i found a little pacifier. i new it couldnt of been mine because im famous in the verdi family for sucking my finger when i was little not my thumb and not a pacifier. when i asked what it was doing there my mom didnt even ask what i was doing looking in her jewelry box she just told me i had a baby sister who died. i asked my sisters name but she woodnt tell me because she said i should ask my dad.

the minute after my mom told me i had a little sister i started wishing she woodnt of died and ive been wishing it ever sense. sure i wished i could of new her and everything and could of had a sister but its not just that. mister curley im not the easiest kid for 2 parents to have. i mean im all special needs in school and my mom has just spent tons and tons of time with me on my school work and they spend a lot of money sending me to saint bernard because of the specialists and everything. also last year i beat that kid up so bad he was in the hospital three weeks and they had to go to a lot of meetings over it and hire lawyers and pay a settlement. isabella wood of been easier to love.

but you know what mister curley ever since yreka brought my flower sack back to me yesterday i just havent been able to get excited about it again. i mean my mom asked if i wanted to bring it to the cemetery today and i said no the 7 days are over im leaving it at home. when we came back she asked what i planned to do with the flower sack now and i said i didnt know because i was finished with the assignment and i didnt want to keep pretending i was responsible for this baby girl but i didnt feel right throwing the flower sack away.

what can you make with 10 pounds of flower i asked and my moms answer was bread.

have you ever baked bread mister curley its enjoyable. my

mom and my dad and i did it together and 1st we dissolved yeast in a little bit of warm water and then we mixed the yeast together with the other ingredients witch are flower salt water and oil. we turned the dough out onto the counter and my mom and dad did all the needing because of my hand and then we left it to rise. we had a lot of dough so we made 4 loves. 1 for our family for dinner tonight. 1 for ricky at the lily pad and of course 1 for arthur and yreka. and 1 for you to say thanks for making me do this assignment and also for reading all my letters. this letter like the 1 before im doing with my left hand only witch takes hours and hours but its worth the trouble.

we put the loves in the oven and my dad went downstairs to his wine cellar and i stayed in the kitchen with my mom.

mom i said how old was i when we moved to cleave springs?

you were a baby she said. your dads grandma died and this house went on the market and he hated the idea of it leaving the family.

did you want to move hear?

i wanted to stay out in the suburbs she said. but he started talking about how he was raised in this house and his dad was raised here too. he wanted to raise his own son here 3 generations and he didnt care that cleave springs was a slum.

its not a slum anymore i said.

no it isnt she said and she was starting to cry. but its still the place where my baby died.

i stayed in the kitchen for a few more minutes and then i went downstairs to the basement and i peeked in threw the doorway and saw my dad holding a glass of wine and smoking a cigar. i raked up all my courage and walked threw the door. when the verdis first came from italy they grew grapes on the land behind our house and used this old wooden press to make wine in our basement. the press is over on one end of the wine cellar and they wood fill it with grapes then put the round wooden lid on it and start cranking it down tighter and tighter and tighter to crush the grapes and squeeze them until there skins cracked open and they gave up there juice.

my dad was surprised to see me but he didnt shoo me away or say anything he just nodded. i wanted to say were you drunk from wine when you rolled over on isabella. i wanted to say mom hates you for it doesnt she. his nose was bruised and thick from me punching it and i wanted to ask if he could smell the baking bread.

my dad got up and took a tall wine glass down from the shelf. he picked up the open bottle and filled the bottom of the glass with dark red wine and then he motioned for me to sit down in the chair next to his and he handed me the glass. i use to taste wine once in a wile when i was a little kid and the verdi family was around on holidays because my relatives were making it look so good. i was always surprised that something that looked so good could taste so awful. now i lifted the glass to my lips and let some of the wine pore into my mouth and held it there for a few seconds before i swallowed. it didnt taste bad like it did when i was younger and it didnt taste good either but it tasted complicated.

one of us had to say something and it wasnt going to be my dad. that swollen nose made his face look gloomy and maybe even in trouble.

dad i said do you know the story of saint bernard.

AIR SPACE

AS SOON AS MOONEY saw her he knew something was wrong. She stood at the top of her porch steps in a sleeveless white nightgown, pale calves and bare feet showing below the hem, slim arms waving, orange hair vivid in the morning light. He paused at the bottom of the wooden steps and Charles and Amelia instantly hairpinned their lean flexible bodies and pointed their snouts back at him, two sets of moist dark eyes hungry for reassurance.

"You don't know, do you?" she said.

"Know what?"

"I can't watch this alone. Can you come inside?"

Before Mooney could answer his neighbor turned around and walked into her house, the nightgown billowing around her legs as his startled mind groped for her name—a name he ought to remember. He had never entered this house before, but for the dogs' sake he acted like it was natural, talking them up the porch stairs and over the threshold.

She stood across the living room, intent on the television he could hear but not yet see. Directly behind her, strong morning sunlight poured in through the window on the east wall of the room. The fabric of the white nightgown was sheer, summer-weight. Before he crossed the room to join her, Mooney accepted the vision that the sun offered him, a clear outline of the woman's profile as if drawn in preparation by an artist who would sculpt her. The form was streamlined, proportional, the small breast above counterbalanced by the slim haunch and modest buttock below. The hair that topped this slender body was spectacular, a persimmon-colored tangle that massed densely upward from the nape of the neck and then roiled above the cranium in an exaltation of sunlit coils. The sun showed Mooney another bank of orange coils flaring forward beneath the gentle rise of her stomach.

On the television screen the Twin Towers were burning. Mooney and his neighbor—he knew her name; he *had* known it—stood side by side watching the spectacle, listening to the newscasters' voices, the dogs whining quietly as they leaned against Mooney's legs.

An explosion curdled the air outside. The dogs squealed and she took hold of Mooney's arm. "What was that?"

They walked together out onto her porch. The street was quiet; the whole neighborhood was quiet. The September sky was blue, the air crisp and warm and still.

"Maman," she said, and they headed back inside.

The phone to her ear, she spoke in rapid French as he stood next to her in front of the television. She stopped talking when the network cut away from the burning towers to report that the Pentagon had been struck.

"That boom," she said to Mooney, and he nodded.

She spoke for a few more minutes and then set down the phone. Newscasters speculated about how many planes had been hijacked, who was flying them, where they would strike next. The dogs lay on the floor, beginning to settle in, but they both jumped to their feet the moment the sirens began to moan. Charles yapped while Amelia tossed her pointed snout skyward and howled. Mooney bent down and stroked Amelia's narrow back.

"What's that?" she said, walking over to the open window.

"What?" Mooney said.

"I smell something."

They went out onto the porch and Mooney smelled it too, something burning, not wood. Something acrid, toxic. Something malignant. She pointed above the roof of the house opposite, and through a gap between the trees he could see the pall of black smoke.

"The Pentagon," he said.

They closed the door and the windows and went back to the television. Sirens wailed from every side of the neighborhood and the dogs answered them. The air in the house grew warm.

"My god," she said, and he realized he'd gotten distracted, was looking away from the television at the pictures on the woman's walls as he rifled through his cluttered mind searching for her name. *Kate? Kathy?*

He looked back at the television in time to see one of the smoking towers crumble and fall in on itself like a pillar of ash. Her hand slid along his lower back and laid hold of his hip. He reached over and pulled her close. They watched as the great clouds of ash and dust billowed among Manhattan's giants. They kept watching as the second tower fell.

"You're crying," she said.

He reached up and touched his wet face. "I can't watch any more of this."

"You're right." She went to switch the television off, then gestured toward the couch. He sat down and she sat next to him, offering a tissue. The next thing he knew they were kissing, not the correct kisses of a first date but the fierce, hungry kisses of people so scared and excited they might try to eat each other. His hands moved over her body frankly, familiarly, as if they were only taking possession of what that first backlit vision of her had promised. Grappling, stumbling, but still kissing, they migrated from the living room into a little hallway and through the door to the sunny bedroom at the back of the house. She flung the nightgown up like a sheet and he shucked his pants as they tumbled onto the bed. He was already inside her when she reached forward to tug his T-shirt over his head. He lay back as she kneaded the flesh over his ribs and ground her hips against his. The orange hair was an aurora on the horizon of his vision. His eyes stayed fixed on the delicate collarbones that flared from her neck like wings.

"Karen!" he shouted, and came.

Eyes closed, he let his untethered mind brew up a storm of translucent tissue paper, tiny squares of it fluttering down from on high, a many-colored blizzard, white, pale yellow, yellow, yellow-orange, orange, red, maroon, purple, Navy blue, royal blue, pale blue, silver, black...

The body on his shifted, brought him back to the moment. He looked over and saw the dogs curled around one another on the runner just beyond the bedroom door. Amelia was the color of cornbread except for the white diamond at her throat. Charles was piebald, white with patches of black. The sirens had stopped. She had been resting her head on his chest but she planted her hands on either side of him now and rose, the tip of her nose hovering no more than an inch from his, her blue eyes difficult to read.

"Who is Karen?" she said.

He shut his eyes. "I was searching for your name the whole time, and then I had it. I thought I did."

"It's Camille."

"Right," he said, opening his eyes again. "Camille Trevor."

She nodded. "Forgive me. I'm just terrible with…"

"Ward Mooney."

"Sorry, Ward. I just think of you as the plane man."

It made sense she would think of him that way. They had first met about a year before, when she had come to his door on a Sunday afternoon and asked him to sign a petition. They spoke on Mooney's porch while he cradled a nearly-finished scale model of the F4U Corsair in his right hand and Charles and Amelia sniffed and whined on the other side of the screen door. He didn't intend to sign her petition. In fact, he had already thrown his support behind the home remodeling project she sought to block.

The home in question stood across the street from Mooney's

place and two houses down. It belonged to Vince Lyle, who shared Mooney's passion for building and flying model aircraft. The Lyles lived in a one-story, two-bedroom bungalow much like Mooney's, but Lyle and his wife had two children, with a third on the way. They needed more space. An engineer, Lyle had bought design software for his home computer and worked up a plan to enclose his house's front porch and add a second story. But the porch of Lyle's 1920s house sat closer to the street than the city's 1950s building codes allowed. To touch that porch, he needed a variance. To get a variance, he had to make an application and notify all the affected neighbors of his intentions. One affected neighbor was Camille Trevor, whose lot backed up to Lyle's.

"What's her deal?" Vince had asked Mooney when he learned from a neighbor that Ms. Trevor was organizing resistance to his plan. Vince's black hair grew in a ring below the bald crown of his head. His scalp was smooth and brown. He had crossed the street with his older child, a boy of six or seven, when he caught sight of Mooney outside waxing his Town Car. "I mean, she can't even *see* my front porch. Why does she care what I do to it?"

Mooney saw Vince's point. A few days later, he signed the counter-petition Vince had drafted. Still, he treated Camille Trevor courteously when she came knocking that Sunday afternoon. He wore a listening expression even if he didn't listen to her all that carefully at first. Nothing she could say would cause him to betray Vince. Besides, he was very much struck by the color of her hair. When her knock sounded, he had been standing at the workbench in his house's second bedroom applying a color almost exactly the same as that of her hair to the tissue-paper skin on his scale model of the F4U Corsair. Around the front of the plane's Navy blue fuselage Mooney was painting flames. He held the Corsair in his hand as he spoke with Ms. Trevor, the fumes from the wet orange paint rising to his nostrils. Before she left, he worked up the nerve to ask her why she was so concerned with the fate of the Lyle porch when she couldn't even see the front of the Lyle house from her own.

"Good question," she said. "I'll answer it with one of my own: where are we standing right now?"

"On my porch," Mooney said.

"Right. We're on your property, under your roof, but not in-side your home. An apt spot for an exchange between neighbors, don't you think?"

The question didn't seem to require an answer.

"May I ask why you bought this house?" she said.

"It was cheap. Convenient to the District, where most of my business is." The sedan he drove for a living, clean and black, sat in the driveway next to the house. He tipped his head in that di-rection.

"Cheap? You've been here a while."

"Ten years," he nodded. "Rougher place when I came in."

"I bought here a year ago," she said. "It wasn't exactly cheap."

"No, not anymore."

"I bought because of the porches," she said, answering the question he hadn't asked as she launched into the lecture on porches that she had been delivering all around the block and would deliver again during the comment period at the Planning and Zoning Commission hearing a few nights hence. Porches, she told him, are not just a homeowner's resource, a place to park the stroller, to leave one's boots on snowy days, to curl up with a book or serve drinks to friends when the weather is fine. Porches are a community resource, a buffer between sidewalk and living room, a place of transition between the public life of the street and the private life of the home. Good porches, she concluded, make good neighbors.

She didn't collect Mooney's signature, but she got his attention. Though he continued to support Vince's plan, to nod sympathetically whenever Vince began to vilify the woman he had begun to call Red, what she had said to Mooney would come back to him that fall whenever he was strolling along a sidewalk with Charles and Amelia and some acquaintance would call out to him from the porch, waving.

AT THE NOVEMBER HEARING, the Planning and Zoning Commission sided with Ms. Trevor and the eleven neighbors who had signed her petition. They told Mr. Lyle to return with a revised design that left the porch unmolested. He did so, and won approval at the Commission's December meeting for the modest second-story addition that he intended to build himself using stockpiled vacation time and weekends.

But the result didn't satisfy Vince. He was a fiery man, a competitor, and anything less than total victory rankled him. This became clear a couple of months later to all the men present at the

February gathering of the Cleave Springs Free Flyers, when the model airplane-related business had been covered and the group members began the social part of their evening. Vince had kept the guys abreast of his renovation project every step of the way. He assumed, rightly, that they would want to see his latest set of blueprints, the third and final version, fresh from the printer. He stood up and uncorked a cardboard tube, rolling his plans out on the rectangular table in the deep room of the Lily Pad, where the club had been gathering the third Wednesday evening of every month for the past six years.

Seven men were present and every one of them stood, jockeying for a clear line of sight as Vince flipped through the rectangular pages, each of which presented a different elevation. The north elevation, the view from the back yard, was the showstopper. Seconds after Vince peeled that page open the whistles and murmurs began to sound.

"You'll show her, won't you Vince?" It was the smoke-charred voice of Pete Bloess, the group's senior member. Pete was seventy-five, a retired civics teacher who wore reading glasses on a leash around his muscular neck. He was saying what everyone thought.

"Show who?" Vince said. The narrow space between his black eyebrows vanished when he squinted.

"How dare she tread on your God-given right to turn your porch into a living room?"

"Not my God-given right, Pete, my American right to do what I want with my property."

Pete cleared his throat. Breathing loudly, he leaned his thick trunk forward and peered down at the blueprint through his glasses. He smiled. "Like turn that little house of yours into a castle?"

"*Castle*," Vince scoffed. He dragged a palm back across his brown pate and began to explain how the octagonal shape of the three-story addition he would build off the back of the house was actually the most practical solution to the problem of maximizing interior space while preserving adequate room outdoors for his kids to play. The ground floor of the octagon would feature a kitchen that was more than half the size of the Lyle family's current dwelling. On the floor above, Vince and his wife Michelle would have the ample master suite that she had dreamt of for years. And on the third floor, beneath the metal-roofed turret that sharpened to a point 70 feet above ground level, Vince would store his tools and tinker with his planes.

"What does the city say?" Pete asked.

"This whole plan is in compliance," Vince said. "They don't much care what I do as long as I leave the porch alone and respect their setbacks."

"Have you shown the neighbor?" one of the younger guys asked. "That chick who lives behind you?"

"Red?" Vince spat, charging the word with the same nasty power it had carried during Mooney's Cold War childhood. "I'm not asking for a variance so I don't have to show her anything. She'll see this when it's built." He swung his head right, then left, smiling. "She'll see it every day."

❖ ❖ ❖

VINCE HAD YET TO BREAK GROUND, a month later, when the Cleave Springs Free Flyers gathered with dozens of other model airplane enthusiasts from the greater metropolitan area for the Capital Challenge, Mooney's favorite event of the year.

Mooney had glued together his first kit model, a dime scale P-47 Thunderbolt, at age eight. Since then, in four decades of focused, passionate work, he had developed a comprehensive knowledge of the aircraft deployed by every nation that engaged in air combat during the two World Wars. His familiarity with body designs, materials, color schemes and insignia was absolute. He accepted model airplane kits as a necessary evil, the low-hanging fruit that kept the hobby robustly populated by dabblers and dilettantes. But his planes were scratch-built all the way. He flew indoors only, unwilling to see months of painstaking labor erased by the kind of sudden gust that can rise up on a calm day, grab hold of a twelve-gram airplane and slam it to smithereens against the trunk of a tree.

There were easier places to fly indoors, but nothing compared with the Great Hall of the National Building Museum for grandeur. This colossal structure occupied most of a city block. Its four floors of office space wrapped around the sides of the Great Hall, a deep rectangular tank that made a reservoir for the light that streamed in through banks of arched windows up near the roof. Two rows of massive Corinthian columns divided the Great Hall into three large square spaces. A circular fountain bubbled in the center square, while the squares on either end of the Hall were reserved on this day for flying. Around the perimeters of these squares, guys knelt over their many-shelved tool boxes while, out on the carpet, other guys stood gazing up at their slowly circling airplanes or cradled the delicate machines against their chests, making minor adjustments and winding the strips of rubber that served as engines. No hot motors allowed.

The vast, still space calmed Mooney and inspired him. He enjoyed the fellowship, too, the great ingathering of kindred spirits with their unkempt hair, their ill-fitting pants and their many-pocketed vests, the great wads of keys clipped to their belt loops. Mooney's job required that he keep his graying chestnut hair and beard carefully clipped, and he had stopped dressing like a dork long ago. Still, this was his tribe, and he had standing among them. As soon as he arrived, guys he'd flown with in the past started coming over to him, asking what he would be flying today. Guys from rival clubs spoke about him in low tones, trying to point discreetly.

Mooney easily won the Peanut class with his 11.5 gram Japanese Zero, a trusty little machine that flew in graceful left-hand circles and stayed in the air sixteen seconds longer than the second-best plane. He sat out the next round, then entered his Fairey Spearfish in the Open Rubber class, which he also won. After that he watched for a while and began to make some last adjustments to his newest creation, the Navy blue Corsair with the orange flames just aft of the prop.

Vince Lyle had set up his toolbox next to Mooney's. He whistled when he saw the Corsair. "What have we here?"

Mooney laid the plane in Vince's open palm. "I'm going to send her up this morning during the trimming session. First time."

Vince studied the plane carefully and then handed it back, envy bleeding into his dark eyes. Vince was the only member of the Cleave Springs Free Flyers with talents that rivaled Mooney's. But Vince spread himself too thin to really excel in any one sector of the hobby. He had a weakness for loud, flashy planes that tore through the sky making gaudy moves he could dictate with a battery-powered remote control. Then too, Vince had the big remodeling project to worry about, a family that took up his time. "Maiden flight?" he said, squinting. "Break a leg."

When the competitive rounds were finished, Mooney strode out onto the carpet as he gave the Corsair's prop a few last turns. He launched the Navy blue bird and watched it begin to climb, light shining down through the translucent tissue, revealing the elegant skeleton as it rose in a widening spiral of left-hand loops. Too wide. The plane crested the arches of the ground-floor arcade in good shape, but nearly clipped the side of a column as it rose above the arcade that gave onto the second-story offices. On the third story there was no arcade, just an open walkway that wrapped around the Great Hall. Mooney lost sight of the Corsair as it sailed over the walkway's parapet.

Oh well. Not bad for a first flight. He was actually glad for the chance to climb up to the third level so he could gaze out over the Great Hall from a high perch. He liked to hike up the building's gently sloping stairs, the dark old bricks grooved and polished by a dozen decades of shuffling feet.

He emerged from the stairwell and peered down the walkway in the direction where the plane had disappeared. The walkway was deserted except for a woman who stood twenty or thirty yards away. Mooney walked toward her, growing concerned as he drew near enough to see that she was holding the Corsair. She did him no favors by picking up the plane. The slightest squeeze in the wrong place could tear the skin or snap a strut, undoing hours of patient toil.

But as he got closer, he saw how gingerly she held the Corsair, how she balanced the plane on the tips of her ten fingers, out away from her body, as she studied it in the rich light that poured through the windows just above. Then he remembered where he'd seen that lively tangle of orange hair before.

She sensed him nearing and shifted her blue eyes away from the plane. "Ah, have you come to fetch this lovely thing?"

"Ward Mooney," he said. "We've met, I believe."

She smiled. "My petition drive. You were holding a plane like this when we talked. Camille Trevor."

Mooney thought of Vince Lyle, who was sorting out the trim of a Grumman Hellcat down below with no idea in the world that his friend might be up here exchanging pleasantries with Red. And then he thought of Vince's addition, the tower that would soon dominate the view from the back windows of this unwitting woman's house.

She handed him the plane. "Did you make it?"

"I did."

"How?"

"Very, very carefully," he said.

She tilted her head, eyeing the plane. "The covering—what kind of paper is that?"

"Japanese tissue. Lightweight, but very strong. The long

fibers shrink when you spray them with water, which makes the skin hold tight to the frame."

"It's wood, the frame?"

"Balsa. The best strength-to-weight ratio available." He could have said more about the wonders of balsa, he could have gone on and on and on, but he caught himself. "Are you here for the Capital Challenge?"

She shook her head. "I work here."

"On Saturdays?"

"Generally, no. We've got a new exhibition opening here next week. The Ethics of Space," she said, smiling. "Kind of a big topic for me, as you may have guessed. Now is crunch time."

"Well, I hope we're not in your way."

"Oh, no. You own this building, Ward. We do. You and me and everyone else down there."

They turned and rested their forearms on the top of the waist-high parapet, light from the arched windows above bathing their faces as they gazed out into the colorful, quiet confusion of circling craft.

ARMORED VEHICLES WITH HEAVY GUNS had taken up positions along the road around the Pentagon. National Airport, minutes from Mooney's house, was closed indefinitely. Roadblocks, barricades, and checkpoints complicated his movements around the edgy District and lengthened drive-times for his passengers. But business was brisk in the days after the attack, the nation's capital swarming with people who dashed about like ants from a kicked nest. They all needed rides, and Mooney was there to drive them.

In the early days, when he still drove for a service, he had gotten used to the night shift. He had worked hard and lived frugally to purchase his independence. In his own car now, master of his schedule, he stuck with what he knew, beginning his workday with the afternoon rush hour and calling it quits at midnight. He ferried lobbyists, Hill staffers and diplomatic people to happy hours, dinner meetings, evening flights and performances, the watering-holes where they went for nightcaps. But this week nobody seemed to be sleeping, and Mooney was rolling in regularly at three.

He would come in exhausted but keyed up, buzzing with the energy of the angry, traumatized capital. He would stroke the dogs for a while, talking them back down into the sleepy state his return had disrupted. He would drink a beer, pull on his pajamas and lie in bed, wondering about Camille Trevor and listening for the new sound in the night sky, the reassuring rumble of the fighter jets that periodically streaked past. The planes up there were the descendents of the ones he replicated, great-grandchildren of the flying machines that crowded the shelves in every room of his house and hung on fishing line from hooks in all the ceilings, their dark forms hovering above him now as he summoned up memories of his younger self, a brown-haired kid curled up in bed, his lamp carving a small circle of light from the general darkness as the dog-eared novel splayed on his pillow wove visions of American fighters dancing to the death with Japanese Zeros and Nazi Messerschmitts, battling evil in far-off places to ensure his safety at home.

Mooney and the dogs passed Camille Trevor's house every

morning and every afternoon. On Tuesday the 18th, as they turned onto her street, it occurred to him that today was an anniversary of sorts. One week. "Who wants to see Camille?" he said to the dogs in an upbeat voice. Charles wagged his tail cautiously while Amelia sniffed the sidewalk. "Okay, let's go see Camille."

He coached them up the porch stairs and kept speaking to them in comforting tones even after he'd knocked on the door. The patter calmed him also.

He half-expected her to be wearing the sheer white nightgown, but she was dressed for the day. She left the door open behind her, stepping out onto the porch in clogs and capris, both dark brown. Her T-shirt was pale blue with a single brown stripe. "Ward," she said.

"Camille."

They shared a smile over the post-coital confusion with names. She lingered comfortably in the moment while he groped for something innocuous to say. At last he managed to ask if she still worked at the Building Museum.

She nodded. "I only go in three days a week. I work from home on Tuesdays and Thursdays. That's why I was here last Tuesday."

They shared a second smile.

"I'm glad you stopped by," she said. "I wasn't sure what to do. I mean, nothing like that's ever happened to me before."

"Me either."

"Listen," she said, losing the fingers of one hand in the depths of her hair. "I'm in the middle of a couple of things right now. Everything is crazy at the museum, all the new security is-

sues. Could you maybe come back later? I could make you dinner."

"I work in the evenings."

"Lunch, then?"

He took the dogs on an extra-long walk. Back home, he
wiped down the inside of the car, cleaned the windows and
shined all the chrome outside. He went to his workbench and
did his best to get involved in a drawing of the Tomahawk Mk 1
he thought he might build. It was hard to concentrate with the
noon hour approaching.

Charles and Amelia were used to him leaving in the late afternoon in his black suit, but seeing him take off at midday in
jeans and T-shirt offended them. They whined at him and pled
with their moist eyes. "*Babies*," he hissed at them. "I'm coming
back."

He did come back, but so late that the dogs' afternoon walk
had to be skipped. He barely had time enough to comb his hair
and knot his necktie before dashing out to the car to begin the
slow drive out to pick up a passenger at Dulles. The smell of
Camille's body made him think of almonds. It lingered in his
beard.

His second visit to the bedroom at the back of her house
had been completely different from the first, things heating up
only after they'd agreed that the unusual circumstances a week
before had only postponed a necessary conversation about birth
control, sexually transmitted diseases, and any personal entanglements that might prevent them from going forward. Camille
was ten months clear of her divorce and not seeing anyone seriously. Mooney had never really *had* personal entanglements. A

lifelong bachelor, he had yet to meet the woman who could pierce the armor of his routines.

The mood was more tentative, more tender this time, more bashful and exploratory, the pace measured. They maneuvered around one another, getting their bearings, kissing a lot, but much to Mooney's satisfaction they arrived at the moment of crisis in the same position he remembered from the first time, Camille poised above him, her hands planted on his chest, her elbows locked, her beautiful collarbones flaring winglike out toward her shoulders as her hair dazzled across the upper edge of his vision.

Afterward they lay in each other's arms and cried. The fear Mooney had felt the morning of the attack, the confusion about what was happening and who was doing it and how bad it might get, crested and broke over him as it had threatened to do all week. He was exhausted from all the late nights, rattled, vulnerable, and he wondered if that was how she felt too.

Camille told him about her mother, a French woman who had married Camille's American father and moved with him to the States fifty years before. She was a widow now, all alone down in Charlottesville, worried about her only child living and working in such a dangerous place.

"I spend the weekends at her house," Camille told him. "You should have seen Maman Sunday afternoon. So distraught. She begged me not to come back here."

FROM THEN ON, Mooney and Camille ate lunch in her kitchen and made love in her bedroom every Tuesday and Thursday. Each time, after he'd dressed, before she began to playfully push him out of the house so she could carry on with her work,

Mooney would stand at the bedroom window and survey the building that was taking shape on the other side of the fence, the white palace with the imposing red-roofed turret that stood twenty feet taller than any other built thing in the vicinity. Camille called it Lyle's Prick.

It was rising very slowly. Over the summer, Vince had wrangled with various cement contractors for weeks before the foundation for the octagonal addition was poured. After framing half of the octagon's first floor, he tore it down and sued the lumber company for selling him bad wood.

The Cleave Springs Free Flyers stopped asking for updates on Vince's project after the attack in September. At the December meeting, once their business was finished, they plunged into a discussion of cruise missile delivery systems and transitioned from there to remote controlled targeting devices and unmanned drones.

Old Pete Bloess interrupted a lively exchange on the wiring of bunker-busting bombs when he uttered a number in his deep, smoky growl: "Twenty-seven-fifty."

"Twenty-seven-fifty," another guy said. "What kind of ordnance is that?"

"It's not a weapon," Pete said. "It's the number of Afghani civilians killed since we started dropping bombs over there. Two-thousand, seven-hundred-fifty. An estimate, of course."

Vince scowled across the table at Pete. "Still not even."

Pete's eyes were level, unblinking. "Even?"

Vince shook his head. "I bet they wish they never agreed to let him hide there."

"These people didn't agree to anything," Pete said.

"You know what I say?" Vince's volume was rising. "I say bombs away. Bomb those fucking mountains and keep bombing until you grind them to sand. And if he's still not killed cross the border and bomb the rest of them."

"Yeah," Pete rumbled, pounding the table with his fist. "I mean, we've got these bombs, we *paid* for the darn things, let's use 'em." He looked around the table hopefully for a moment, then shook his head. "That was supposed to be a joke."

Mooney and Vince walked home from the Lily Pad together, as usual, and they were quiet until they reached Vince's driveway, which had become a source of much grumbling in the neighborhood. The driveway was crowded with tarp-covered building supplies. A rusted tricycle, upside down, anchored one corner of the blue fabric. A half-used pile of gravel spilled off one side of the slab into the weedy flower bed. A thick layer of mud covered the whole surface, leaching out across the sidewalk and clogging the gutter.

Mooney asked how the project was going and Vince launched a rant about the neighbors, how they'd been calling behind his back to bring inspectors out, how someone had dumped yogurt on Michelle's car and someone else had cut one of his extension cords.

"The calls don't surprise me," Mooney said. "But vandalism?"

"You think I'm lying?"

"I didn't say that."

"They're just pissed," Vince said, reflective. "They beat me down on enclosing the porch, but they couldn't stop my addition.

It's bitterness, plain and simple. But I'll tell you what, Ward, it's going to be so sweet when I finish. I've got it all framed up now, got the house wrap on the exterior walls and the roof up on the tower." He cuffed Mooney firmly on the shoulder. "But I don't need to tell *you* how things are going back there."

Mooney's throat went dry. He had been meeting Camille for three months now, three solid months, but they were not a public couple. They took no measures to conceal their relationship but they also did nothing that would attract attention. Their schedules only allowed them to meet on those Tuesday and Thursday afternoons, when most everybody in the neighborhood was off at work or school.

But that was it. Vince went inside, Mooney went home, and by the time he had put on his pajamas he had almost convinced himself that Vince didn't know about him and Camille, that his comment and the little blow to the shoulder were innocuous, that Mooney was making Vince's words seem to say more than they actually did.

Next morning, as Mooney descended the porch steps, trying to keep the dogs' leashes untangled, something out of sorts registered at the edge of his vision and caused him to look over at his Town Car. It was sitting too low. He and the dogs slowly circled the car, but the lap they took was largely ceremonial. He could see before they began it that the tires had been slashed.

MOONEY TOLD CAMILLE ABOUT THE TIRES that afternoon. They had finished making love, he had dressed, but instead of going over to the window, he sat on the side of the bed and watched

her pulling her clothes back on. Mooney was rattled. Except for
the lack of blood, the absence of physical pain, this act of ag-
gression had struck him like a physical assault, as if some thug
had chopped off four of his toes.

The news didn't even seem to surprise Camille. "You're a
traitor," she said. "Do you expect to go unpunished?"

"If I'm seeing you, how is that his business?"

"That's how neighborhoods work," she said, zipping up her
jeans. "The lines around these lots are blurry."

"You're defending him?"

"I don't defend terrorists." She smiled—not at her choice of
words, Mooney saw, but at his naïvete. "Poor Plane Man. You
helped a neighbor in need during a national emergency. This is
the thanks you get?"

"I don't need to be thanked."

"No, you just have to accept that nothing happens in a vac-
uum. Each of your actions resonates. One thing leads to another." She sat down next to him on the edge of the bed.
"Speaking of which, you've been having lunch with me for—
what—three months now? I hope you don't think you can avoid
meeting Maman."

He was too busy brooding over the tires to ask what she had
in mind. Anyhow, she would let him know when the time came.

IT CAME ONE DAY in early March, as they sat together in her
kitchen over bowls of minestrone. She proposed a weekend together in Charlottesville. Mooney resisted the idea not just because he would miss a night of work but also on account of the

dogs. He had adopted Charles and Amelia through a whippet rescue program. They were fragile creatures, he explained, survivors of abuse. They depended on him.

The next time they met Camille told him about an intern at the Building Museum, very experienced with dogs, who had offered to spend the weekend with Charles and Amelia.

"A stranger?" Mooney said, his head shaking dubiously.

Now that he and Camille had a routine it was not uncommon for short conversations to sprout up and briefly interrupt their sex. The next time Camille brought up Charlottesville Mooney was sitting cross-legged on the middle of her mattress and she was sitting in the triangular space between his thighs, her legs folded around his back.

"Plane Man," she said. "I have an idea about Charles and Amelia."

"An idea?"

"We'll bring them along."

"No," he said, stiffening.

"Maman likes dogs."

She rocked forward and reached down, slipping him inside.

"That car is my livelihood," Mooney said. "I can't haul dogs in it."

She closed her eyes, working her hips from side to side. Her brow furrowed. "Who said anything about *your* car?"

ON A SATURDAY MORNING in late April they laid towels across the back seat of Camille's Subaru and Mooney lured Charles and Amelia into the wagon with little balls of raw hamburger. The dogs were either calmed by the motion of the car or sunk in a fearful stupor. They slept for all but the first five minutes of the two-hour drive and awoke when Camille pulled to a stop in the parking lot at Monticello.

The day was mild and breezy, the sky busy with bright white clouds that occasionally blocked the sun. The big trees around Thomas Jefferson's hilltop manor were just leafing out. Mooney took Amelia and let Camille hold Charles' leash. They walked all over the grounds. At the edge of the west lawn, near a planting of larkspur, they paused so Amelia could pee. They gazed across the lawn at the house, its white dome hovering beyond the pillared portico. Mooney compared the living-color version to the one on the back of the nickel he'd fished from his pocket.

Camille sighed. "I look at this place, and it doesn't say *mansion* to me."

"What does it say?"

"A word Vince Lyle should learn—*scale*. I have no beef with big houses, Plane Man. They can be lovely, like this one, if they're in the right context and have enough space around them. Vince's problem is that he wants a palace on a postage stamp, and so what if he trashes the architectural integrity of the neighborhood. So what if he wrecks his neighbors' view."

"I think that's part of the point," Mooney said.

"Speaking of Vince," Camille said a little later, as they drove down the hill, "did you hear Michelle's leaving?"

Vince had stopped coming to Free Flyers meetings, and Mooney hadn't heard anything about him in months. Vince's wife was close with Camille's next-door neighbor; they talked on the phone every couple of days. As soon as the school year ended Michelle was going to her parents' place in upstate New York and taking the kids with her.

"You can't blame her," Camille said. "While Vince works on the palace, they're living in a space that's half the size of the original house, cooking on a hotplate, washing dishes in the bathtub. The kids can't play outside because the job site's hazardous. Plus, Vince is a creep. Michelle has just had it."

"Will she come back at the end of the summer?"

"Vince better hope so. That's a lot of house for one ridiculous man."

The dogs were wide awake for this ride, whining and trembling in the back seat. Mooney reached back and stroked them as Camille drove into town.

The house she had grown up in was a gray Cape Cod that sat on a quiet street three blocks from the University of Virginia, where her father had taught. A pair of healthy ferns hung from the eve of the front porch.

"Your first porch?" Mooney said as they climbed the steps.

"We wouldn't have survived my adolescence without it," Camille laughed. She pointed toward the swing that hung from chains at the far end. "Cordless didn't exist yet, so I'd pass the phone to myself through the window. That swing was my spot."

Maman opened the door in her apron, saying they were just in time for the meal. Her lead-gray hair was long and straight, gathered up at the back of her head in a loose bun. Her eyes were steady and dark.

It smelled wonderful inside. She sat them at the square dining

room table and served carrot soup first, then roast duck with potatoes, then salad. Mooney rarely drank during the day, but the
wine was so good he had a second glass. The conversation was
easy, mostly about the weather, the traffic on their trip down.
Mooney only heard Maman's accent because he was listening for
it. From time to time she would peek beneath the table to say
kind things to the dogs.

After the cheese, as they sipped coffee and ate pear tart, the
old woman reached over and placed her warm hand on top of
Mooney's. "Ward, may I ask you something?"

He waited.

"Does it worry you, living there?"

"In Cleave Springs?" he said. "Not at all."

"But the attack. It came so close."

"Our air space is safer now than it's ever been," he said.
"Think about it. We live under the same umbrella as the president."

Maman grimaced slightly, removing her hand from his.
"Camille says the District is different. Less…"

"Less free," Camille said in the decisive tone that Mooney
usually admired.

"Maybe," he said, feeling his face grow warm. "But more
safe."

Mooney thought he saw the two women exchange a look before Camille got up to clear. While mother and daughter did the
dishes and conversed in French, he wandered around the house
with Charles and Amelia in tow. Books took up most of the wall
space, but there were also a few family pictures that told Mooney

where Camille's coloring had come from. The father was pale, blue-eyed, with a froth of strawberry-blond hair. In one photo—Mooney guessed it was twenty years old—the professor and Camille stood side by side in academic robes, faces celebratory, hair swirling out from under the black tassled hats on their heads. The only time Mooney had ever donned a mortar board was when he finished high school.

Maman needed a nap, so Mooney and Camille took the dogs for a walk around the campus Jefferson had plotted at the foot of the little mountain that gave his house its name. They began at the south end of the terraced lawn and walked up the gentle slope until they reached the white-roofed rotunda that stood in the background of the graduation photo he had seen back at the house. On the rotunda steps, they sat and stroked the dogs, looking out over the long reach of grass.

"The ethics of space," Camille said. "Jefferson wanted to design buildings that embodied civic virtues. Do you think that's possible?"

Mooney was slightly drunk, and still a bit bothered by the way the dessert conversation had ended. "Why not concentrate on people?" he said.

She smiled. "You sound just like my father. 'We need to design *people* who embody civic virtues. Who cares where they live and study?' That was his line. We used to go around and around about it. Maman agreed with me that there was a connection. I wish Dad was alive to see Vince's house. That might've convinced him."

The professor was ten years dead, but his study remained as

he had left it, the pipe in the ashtray, the chair parked at the desk
as if awaiting his return from a weekend away. Camille's old room
had a double bed for guests. After dinner, Mooney took some
time getting the dogs settled in the living room and then went to
the guest room to put on his pajamas. He lay in bed listening to
the rising and falling tones of Camille and Maman. Camille had
gone to say goodnight thirty minutes before.

When she finally came to bed she was in the summer-weight
nightgown she had worn the morning they first made love.
"Hasn't this been a strange day?" she said.

"Strange?"

"I was realizing up at Monticello that you and I have barely
been outside with each other. And now here we are, Tuesday-
Thursday lovers for eight months, about to spend our first night
together. It's exciting, Plane Man." She turned off the lamp and
rolled over to him.

They kissed for a few minutes, but then she rolled away and
turned the light back on. "You're not excited."

Mooney gazed at the ceiling. "You really think we're less
free?"

"And not necessarily more safe, as they would have us believe."

"But they caught us off guard that one time," he said. "Now
we're vigilant. The element of surprise is gone."

"Don't take this the wrong way," she said, "but I believe we
can't live without the element of surprise. Think about it. Would
you and I have connected if I hadn't been half-naked on my
porch that morning, flagging you down?"

He didn't answer.

"Admit it, Ward, you were surprised. Your defenses were down."

"What *were* you doing out there?" he said.

"I was terrified. I couldn't stand to be alone. I rushed out to the porch, and here you came up the sidewalk. A familiar face. The plane man." She nuzzled up close to him, her breath warm on his neck.

"Your mother must wonder what you see in me," he said, still looking at the ceiling.

"She doesn't have to wonder. I've told her."

"Told her what?"

"About Charles and Amelia. And your planes." She lifted her head and reached over to stroke his beard with the backs of her fingers. "When we bumped into each other at the Building Museum that time, I asked how you'd made the plane I found. You said, 'Very, very carefully.'"

"I remember."

"Let's just say I haven't always chosen careful men."

OLD PETE BLOESS was sick. He missed the May meeting of the Cleave Springs Free Flyers, calling Mooney to tell him he was having some health troubles but would definitely be there in June. But before the June meeting, Pete's wife called Mooney to say Pete was going to have to stop coming.

Otherwise the summer went well—until August, when Camille left to spend a month in France with Maman. She had invited Mooney to join them, but he had declined. Knowing he'd made the right decision—the only decision that would keep his bills paid and his dogs sane—didn't help him navigate the middle of every Tuesday and Thursday while she was away. The Tomahawk Mk 1 was finished. He had planned to use the extra time to get started on the next plane, but when he went to his workbench he had a hard time getting excited about something new.

The third Tuesday of the month, he decided to go pay Pete Bloess a visit. The heat outside was awful. He walked the six blocks to Williams Street and arrived at Pete's house with a soaked shirt and beads of sweat rolling down his legs.

Ida Bloess answered the door and led Mooney into the cool house. In the living room, a news channel played on the television and Pete dozed in a big chair with a blanket over his legs. His color was bad. Skin hung like gathered curtains on either side of his wasted neck.

Ida muted the television. She touched Pete's arm and Mooney watched him struggle like a man rising from deep water.

"Ward." The voice was weak. "Lung cancer. It's bad."

"Ida told me." Mooney offered Pete the plane he had brought, a B-26 Invader like the one he had flown in Korea.

Pete took the plane and looked it over carefully before setting it on the table beside his chair. "Ward, your planes always made me feel like I had too many thumbs. Beautiful work. Thanks for stopping by."

"We miss you," Mooney said. "The club isn't the same."

"I miss you guys too," Pete said. "Did Vince ever come back?"

"No."

"Those two younger guys?"

"They followed Vince's lead, I guess."

"Well, that's my fault. I must've pushed back on Vince a little too hard. Just couldn't stomach all that war mongering."

"Actually," Mooney said, "it's not your fault." He told Pete about himself and Camille.

"Consorting with the enemy," Pete said, nodding.

Mooney considered gossiping about Vince's marital troubles, but thought better of it. "About the club," he said. "With our numbers as low as they are, I'm wondering if we shouldn't maybe merge with another club. The Cloudbusters up in Rockville are really solid in every sector of the hobby. I know the guy who runs that outfit pretty well. I thought I'd bring it up at the meeting tomorrow night."

"Makes sense," Pete said. "But it's sure too bad. What we had there, that group of guys, all of us living right here in Cleave Springs—we were a community. That's what kept me coming back. You probably noticed I lost interest in the planes."

"Your arthritis?"

"That was my excuse. But the fact is the hobby started to bother me. I flew in a warplane, Ward. I know what they're made for. I was no pacifist back in Korea, but I guess the seed got planted there. It's been growing ever since. How do you reconcile that with a hobby that glorifies killing machines?"

"I guess I don't think of them that way," Mooney said. "I'm so involved in making calculations, drawing plans, shaving balsa, cutting paper, thinning enamels. I can't get past how fragile they are."

"Even the real ones are fragile. Fragile and deadly."

Mooney sneezed. The convulsion came so suddenly he failed to cover his nose.

"Bless you," Pete said.

Mooney checked his watch. "I'd better get going."

Pete raised his hands and Mooney reached out to take them in his own. They were surprisingly light, as if he had balsa for bones. "Ward," he said, "I'm glad to hear you've got someone to love." His eyes went to the television across the room and Mooney's eyes followed, seeing the president stride across the White House lawn toward a waiting helicopter, his jaw firmly set and his jacket flapping in the wind. Something or someone caught the Commander-in-Chief's attention and he broke his stride to glance backward, tangling his feet in the maneuver, and nearly falling flat on his face before he flung his arms out for balance and wobbled through a series of lunging steps. Walking normally again, he reached down quickly to brush a small chunk of turf off the knee of his slacks, doing his best to reassemble his resolute expression, to act as if the stumble had never occurred.

"You'll need it," the old man softly growled.

MOONEY ATTENDED PETE BLOESS'S FUNERAL on September 7th, a Saturday. Four days later, on the 11th, Camille took the morning off and she and Mooney spent it together in bed. They pleased each other—they knew very well how to please each other by now—but on this day, this anniversary of their first fantastic coupling, the current running between them was a faint reminder of the energy that had crackled in this same house 365 days before.

Afterward they lay spent, side by side on the bed with the bunched top sheet snaking through their limbs. "Thank you for this year," Camille said.

"Thank *you*."

"The right thing for me, at the right time."

"Me too."

She propped herself up on an elbow. "We can't be Tuesday-Thursday lovers forever, Plane Man. I can't." When he didn't say anything she took his chin in her hand and turned his face toward her. "Could you?"

"What kind of lovers do you want to be?" he asked.

"I don't know. The off the clock kind, I suppose."

"Off the clock," he said. "What would that look like?"

She rolled up onto him and held her face just above his, hovering. "Stay tuned."

In early November, Camille told Mooney that Maman was moving to France, to an old stone house in the Normandy town where she had been raised. Camille was going with her, and they wanted him to join them.

Before he could begin to explain how impossible that was she quoted the outrageous figure he could expect to sell his bungalow for, explained that Maman already owned the charming and spacious stone house they would share, described in detail the procedure for shipping dogs safely across the Atlantic, and assured him that the model airplane hobby was alive and well in France.

"This is about more than a T-shirt," Mooney said, referring

to a shirt Maman had seen a man wearing at the supermarket a week or so before. It said:

FIRST IRAQ
THEN FRANCE

Camille smiled. "We've been talking seriously since August. Maman kept bringing it up last year, so we decided to go there for a month and see how it felt."

"She wants to finish her life there?"

"That's part of it. Also, she's just ready to get out of here."

"She's scared?"

"We both are. But not like we were when it first happened."

"What are you scared of?"

"This country's on the warpath," Camille said. "People are *buying* those T-shirts."

"You'd move across the ocean because of *them*?"

"Maman has to do this," she said. "I can't let her go alone. Besides..."

"Besides?"

Camille tilted her head. "You and me, there? Who knows..."

MOONEY KNEW BETTER than to try talking Camille out of something once her mind was set. With him or without him, she was going to France. He agreed to go along. Camille and Maman hadn't yet picked a departure date. In fact, there seemed to be no big hurry to leave, which suited Mooney just fine.

But then Camille was offered a job at an architectural library in Rouen—an easy commute from the stone house. They wanted her to start the first of the year. Camille accepted the job and Mooney smothered his misgivings in activity, helping her pack up the house and get it ready for the market. She showed it on a Sunday in mid-December and the bidding war raged all day Monday. Tuesday morning, she accepted an offer that was forty thousand dollars above an asking price that Mooney had thought laughably high.

Maman joined them in Cleave Springs for Christmas. Charlottesville now had a reputation as a good place to raise kids and young couples were flocking there to breed. Her house had sold for a big sum also. She had donated the professor's books to the university library, sold off the furniture, and shipped the rest of her belongings to France. Her gift to Mooney was a set of French language CDs.

Maman and Camille prepared a sumptuous holiday meal in Mooney's spartan kitchen, and the three of them ate in his dining room.

"When did you come to the States?" Mooney asked Maman.

"1950," she said, glancing up toward the planes that hovered above the table. "Not long after the war."

"What was it like, changing countries?"

Maman set down her fork. "I've always found this country attractive, though at times it has discouraged and frightened me. I was here for Civil Rights, Vietnam, a great deal of upheaval. Frankly, I've never found it as repellent as I do now."

"I promise you," Mooney said, sounding to himself like a salesman whose customer is about to walk, "you're safe here."

She reached over and placed her warm hand on his, just as

she had when he'd sat at her table. "None of us is ever completely safe, Ward. I accept that. For now, I prefer to be under threat elsewhere."

Mooney loaded his Town Car's trunk with luggage and drove Camille and Maman to Dulles the next morning. Camille's dark wool hat covered most of her hair and the boots she wore made her taller than usual. After they checked in, Maman joined the security line alone, giving Camille and Mooney a moment of privacy.

Camille hugged him tightly, pressing her body against his in a way that made his groin tingle. "It's better this way," she said.

"Better than what?"

"This is just forcing you to decide."

"You've decided?"

"Only that I'm open to trying this. There's no guarantee it will work." She brushed his beard with the backs of her fingers and he grabbed her hand roughly in his. "*Ouch!*"

"You're torturing me," he said.

Tears sprang from her eyes. "I'm *what?*"

He released her hand and scanned the security line until he caught sight of Maman, who was having a heated exchange with a security person just beyond the metal detector. "Go help your mother."

HE HAD TOLD CAMILLE his launch would have to wait until after the Capital Challenge in March. He needed time to sort through everything he had accumulated in the house over the years and get the place ready to sell. Also he wanted to fly in the Building

Museum one last time. Joining the Cloudbusters, the model air-plane group in Rockville, had renewed his zeal for the hobby. The drive to Rockville was bothersome, but a couple of the guys in the Cloudbusters were purists like Mooney. They had admired him from afar over the years and now wanted to learn as much as they could from him. Mooney was a mentor, a bit of a star.

Through the first two months of the year, when he wasn't driving, sleeping, or walking the dogs, he was working like a demon on a SPAD S.XIII that he planned to unveil at the Capital Challenge. The SPAD S.XIII was a French-made biplane of World War One vintage. Other countries had flown the SPAD S.XIII, but Mooney planned to apply the French tri-color insignia to the rudder and fuselage in honor of Camille. He would tell her all about the biplane whenever they spoke on the phone, and she would listen attentively before she began to ask how it was going with the house. He told her he had given most of his planes away to guys in the new club. His French? The language discs, he said, lived on the front seat of the car, going into the player whenever he was between clients. He talked as though that last moment at the airport had never happened and she also let it lie.

Until the Friday afternoon before the Capital Challenge. She called at 3 o'clock, wanting to catch him before he started his shift. "What was it that T-shirt said? First Iraq...?" Three days before, U.S. bombs and cruise missiles had begun destroying targets in Baghdad.

"We're not going to attack France," he said.

"Anyway, I called to wish you good luck tomorrow. Will you fly the blue one with the flames?"

"The Corsair? I thought I would."

"I remember the day it landed at my feet."

"Two years ago."

"I'll never forget the look on your face when you saw me holding your plane."

"Most people would have damaged it."

"Do you know you broke my hand?" she said.

"Your hand?"

"Only one bone. A little fracture. It's almost healed now."

This information sucked the air right out of him. He wanted to apologize but the breath wouldn't come.

THE GREAT HALL was as serene as Mooney remembered it, air smoothing the edges of every sound and light softening any surface it touched. He placed his toolbox near the rest of the Cloudbusters and set up the planes he had brought on the club's table. A steady stream of admirers passed the table to ogle the SPAD S.XIII as he stood on the carpet watching his little Zero circle higher and longer than any other plane in the Peanut class. With a nostalgic lump in his throat, he flew the Navy blue Corsair with the orange flames in the Open Rubber class and won that handily also.

There was time to kill before the trimming session, when he'd have a chance to send the new SPAD up for its maiden flight, so he decided to hike up the stairs and have a look at everything from above. He retraced the steps that had taken him to Camille two years before, but when he emerged onto the third-story walkway no orange-haired beauty with exquisite collarbones awaited him. The only person up there was a balding guy with a fringe of dark hair who was leaning out over the parapet and watching the planes.

"Vince," Mooney said.

Vince turned and squinted, his two eyebrows becoming one. "Ward."

"I didn't see you on the floor."

"Too busy to work on my planes," Vince said. "Didn't want to miss the event so I came up here to watch."

Side by side, they leaned their forearms on the parapet and gazed out at the circling craft. "We still have the best ones in the world," Vince said. Mooney had been waiting for someone to say it, preparing himself to hear what followed, the idea that had comforted him all his life, the umbrella he had hunkered under so long that even now, after he had seen the darkness through its holes, he couldn't bring himself to move out from under it. "That's why you and I can stand in this peaceful place today while our guys unleash ten kinds of hell over there."

Mooney remembered the explosion, the way the air curdled around Camille's house.

"I guess you know Michelle and I are finished," Vince said.

"I'm sorry." He recalled the pall of black smoke that rose into the blue September sky, the fearful smell of the burning wreckage.

"The remodel was hard on us, Ward. Here I thought I was making us a dream place to live, and I went and drove her away. I keep thinking if she'd just come and see it, she'd change her mind. It's almost finished now. I don't mean to brag, but it's sweet. The first million dollar house on the street. That's what my realtor says."

The sirens. Charles' manic yapping and Amelia's howls. "Your realtor?"

Vince nodded. "I'm selling the place as soon as it's completely done. Divorce isn't cheap. Besides, there couldn't be a better time to put it on the market. This war on terror has been great for the economy around here. You see it, Ward. What people are paying for houses in Cleave Springs is unbelievable."

Beads of sweat poured across Mooney's ribs. His throat was parched. "Where will you go?"

"Got my eye on a piece of property in West Virginia. Twenty acres. I can build a house on it and still clear two-hundred grand. Even better, there's plenty of space between me and the neighbors."

He couldn't silence the noises in his ears, couldn't expel that smell from his nostrils.

"Speaking of which," Vince said, "I heard through the grapevine that Red moved to France."

"Camille."

"Right. You going to follow her?"

"I may," Mooney lied, and then told Vince he had to go. He walked back to the stairs and hurried down the six flights to the floor, where he gathered up his toolbox and planes. He left without speaking to anyone.

The streets were wide open on this Saturday afternoon, no war protesters in sight, Mooney cruising swiftly through the city that gave him his living, the capital of the free world, its broad avenues lined with marble facades, its narrow side streets pocked with holes. This peaceful place.

Six minutes to the river, six more to his driveway. He entered the house and the dogs whined happily at their protector's return, sniffing his legs as he walked around the rooms, the three of them surrounded by the killing machines that still lined all the shelves, still crowded the air space beneath all the ceilings.

Eventually he sat down on the couch, propping a foot on the coffee table where the package of CDs sat unopened. "Fools," he said, looking into Amelia's moist dark eyes, then Charles' eyes, then back at Amelia. "Lucky fucking fools."

RIGHT OF WAY

UP THE SIDEWALK the two of them came, the boy ugly, the cat beautiful. Nita judged them an odd couple, opposites attached. The cat—a sleek calico, white with patches of orange and black—veered up the driveway toward her and she knelt to pet it. The boy slunk past.

"Pretty cat," she ventured.

The boy kept going, as if he hadn't heard, which gave her a chance to change her mind, to think better of reaching out to him. But she recognized something in his abject posture, a mood she felt from time to time but had stopped seeing in the mirror in the weeks since she'd begun to show. On her, pregnancy was a persona, a disguise.

It had gotten predictable. All the way across the country, at every stop, the fellow motorists she encountered, the gas station attendants, the convenience store cashiers and coffee shop waitresses and motel clerks—all of them had smiled versions of the same upbeat smile, reflecting back the glow she gave off, no matter how awkward or scared or snotty she might feel. No matter how displaced.

"Hello there," she said louder, and the boy stopped, turned. "Your cat. What's her name?"

He shrugged.

Nita stood up and the cat rubbed its side against her ankles. "We could use some help here. Would you like to make some money?"

The boy leaned to the side and peered behind her, like she might be hiding someone. His gaze shifted onto her occupied belly. After all, she had said *we*.

She gestured with her thumb toward the stuffed U-HAUL parked in the driveway behind her. "My husband and I just drove this truck from California. We're new to the neighborhood. I'm Nita." She stepped forward, willing her hand to rise and open and touch that fish-belly skin.

Wright saved her. She slowed down when she heard him bustle out the front door and down the steps. He strode past her, reached the kid first and clasped the limp hand.

"I'm Wright," he said to the boy, and Nita's eyes shut in anticipation of the joke that came next. "Even when I'm wrong."

The boy watched the cat jog down the driveway and across the street. Dank hair hung like seaweed from his head.

"Wright is his name," Nita explained, pulling the boy's eyes back to her. "What's yours?"

"Ash." The voice was clear and high, crisp as a struck bell.

"Nita's named after a tree, too," Wright said. "A shrub, actually. Manzanita? It grows out West."

"How much?" the boy said.

Wright was the only man Nita knew who smiled when he

was confused. She found this lovable. "Oh," he said, "it grows pretty profusely in dry regions. It's drought tolerant."

Nita put her hand on Wright's shoulder. "How much will we pay, he means."

"God," Wright laughed, "I don't know. What's a fair price, Ash?"

They studied the boy's face for evidence of silent calculations.

"Why don't we see how long it takes and then figure it out," Nita finally said. "Don't worry, Ash, we'll make it worth your while."

"Sure we will," Wright said. "We're used to Bay Area prices."

If not for Bay Area prices, Nita's little collection of hand-blown glass objects would be catching the morning light on a windowsill in Oakland right now, not swaddled in newspaper and nestled among packing chips in a crowded cardboard box. If not for Bay Area prices, she would have been drinking seltzer on her parents' deck as the sun set behind Mt. Tamalpais yesterday evening, not talking to them on the phone from the empty living room of an ugly little brick house surrounded by weedy flower beds. One listen to Mom's foggy purr, Dad's wry laugh, and she knew they'd already smoked their evening joint. So their first grandchild would be born three thousand miles away. No reason to panic.

She guessed Ash was thirteen or fourteen. Pinched shoulders, limbs like hanger wire, but still plenty strong enough to help Wright wrangle the heavier boxes, the mattress, and the few pieces of furniture from the truck. They set the lighter boxes aside for Nita to carry.

Nita's nose, sensitive since the pregnancy's first days, told her more about Ash than she wanted to know. His odor included scalp oil, sweat, stale smoke, and substantial amounts of plain dirt—a tamer mixture of the stench that leapt from the street people she was used to passing on Telegraph Avenue. There was another element as well, something dank and sewery that she couldn't quite place. The whole house reeked of him.

Nevertheless, she was determined to feed him before he left. The truck was mostly unpacked when she went into the kitchen to fix some lunch. She pulled out the cold cuts and fruit that she'd unpacked from the travel cooler last night. She made more sandwiches than three people should be able to eat and set them out with fruit and potato chips on the square wooden table she'd bought at the Berkeley flea market several years before. She had stripped and refinished the table herself and it soothed her to have it here.

Little Hoover was Wright's nickname for the fetus—such was the rapacity the growing creature stoked in Nita. Ash ate the way Nita *wanted* to eat. He hunched forward and wolfed the food fiercely, downing half-sandwiches with quick double-bites, gnashing chips, gobbling handfuls of grapes and clearing the salt and juice from his face with swipes of his grimy arms.

Nita had opened all the windows the minute she got her first whiff of Ash. After paying the boy, Wright came in and found the little fan they'd brought. He set it up in the front doorway and turned it on high, looking to flush the house with fresh air sucked in through the back. Nita stood on the front steps, feet spread and hands on hips, taking deep breaths. The queasiest weeks were behind her now, but the fetus could still be fickle. With each exhalation, she urged Little Hoover not to evict the lunch.

"So," Wright said, joining her. "Ash."

That second syllable, released into the funky air the fan forced out, triggered a moment of truth. Nita bent over the edge of the step and surrendered her food to the weeds.

HE LIVED NEXT DOOR to Wright and Nita's place, in a two-story yellow-brick building with mold and ivy growing on its walls and rotten wood trim around its windows and doors. A crenelated parapet surrounded the flat roof, creating a haunted-castle effect.

There were two apartments in the building. The young woman on the first floor spent a lot of time on the sagging front porch. Nita figured Ash lived upstairs. The only other person she ever saw come and go from the building was a grizzled man who occasionally shuffled out or in wearing the spattered white clothes of a professional painter. The man trod gingerly in the mornings, as if his whole body hurt. He careened like a storm-tossed dinghy whenever she saw him late in the day.

The school bus stopped just up the street and Nita saw Ash get off it every weekday afternoon even after the summer break began for most kids. He had no backpack, but he sometimes toted a plastic grocery bag. Other kids would tumble off the bus in a gaggle, laughing and teasing each other. Ash was always alone. Most days, he'd veer off the sidewalk and head up the edge of the old railroad right of way that cut a diagonal green strip through the heart of Cleave Springs. The city had turned most of this right of way into parkland. The section across the street was a playground. Dog owners exercised their pets in the section that ran along the east side of Wright and Nita's lot. The dog area continued for a good hundred yards and ended at a rusty metal fence topped with barbed wire. A thick chain secured the gate in the middle of this fence, but there was enough slack in the chain that Ash could crouch down and slip through the opening in one fluid, furtive motion.

Peering from the edge of her yard, Nita watched him slip through on several different occasions before she asked Wright what lay beyond the fence.

"More right of way, according to the map. It goes on for another half-mile and ends at the highway."

"Why is it closed off?" she asked, actual curiosity fortified by her desire to keep him at the dinner table. Renovation drawings occupied him every evening now that all the boxes were unpacked and the walls inside wore fresh paint.

"I'm guessing the homeowners whose lots back up to it asked the city to do that."

"For security?"

"Probably. The pioneer mentality."

"What do you think it's like back there?"

"There's one way to find out," he said, rising from the table. "Let's go take a look."

In the dog area this evening, a young couple were exercising a big chocolate Lab. The guy, in his office shirt and tie, threw a tennis ball for the dog while the woman swayed from side to side, soothing the baby in her sling.

Wright and Nita held hands and picked their way along the edge of the dog area. Cicadas sawed in the branches above, a sound that grated in her western ears. They arrived at the fence and peered through a narrow section that wasn't completely strung with vines. The terrain beyond the fence was uneven, with clumps of thick vegetation growing here and there and the back-yard fences of the first houses visible. Wright went to the gate and pulled it toward him until the chain grew tight. The gap was bigger than she had imagined—wide enough to admit not just a skinny boy, but also a pregnant woman. Passing feet had worn the ground beneath it bare.

"Shall we?" he said.

"Not now."

He smiled. "You scared?"

She had seen Ash slide through several hours before and thought he might still be in there. "If they wanted people going back there, why would they put up a fence?"

Wright stepped back and appraised the fence a moment, his face tipped slightly skyward, regarding not the thing that stood in front of him but a quickly-forming vision of what that thing might one day become. The architect gaze, Nita called it.

"There's no need for this fence anymore. It's got to come down." He turned and looked back the way they'd come. "That bike path along the right of way doesn't have to stop at the play-ground. It could come up along the edge of this dog section and continue right through here to the highway. Before you know it, you're riding on the path along the river."

He fell quiet then, savoring this vision of connectedness.

"What was that?" Nita said. She thought the baby in the sling had cried out, but when she turned to look the young parents and their chocolate Lab were gone.

"You heard something?"

"A cry. Didn't you hear it?"

"All I hear is cicadas."

She stepped back up to the fence and looked through the opening in the vines. Ash stood between two clumps of bushes less than twenty yards in, the skin of his face and his bare arms luminous in the failing light. He held what looked like a half-empty jug of milk in one hand. Gazing directly at her, he raised the finger of his free hand and pressed it to his lips. She turned back to Wright.

"See anything?" he said.

A strange urge to protect the boy made her answer Wright opaquely. "It sounded like a child."

Wright turned back the way they'd come and Nita sent one quick, searching look through the fence before she stepped away. Ash was gone.

On the way back to the house, Wright talked with great excitement about how close Cleave Springs sat to the greenbelt along the Potomac. The way this place linked them to the city and its hinterlands, to culture and nature and history, was one of the things he loved best about the neighborhood he'd chosen. For Cleave Springs was his choice. He had picked it on a scouting mission he'd conducted in the early spring, after his final interview with the Washington firm whose opening he'd filled.

Nita had never expected to settle so far away from her home ground. San Francisco Bay, and the hills and valleys ringing it, formed a big bowl that contained her whole life except for the past few weeks. Her parents had set up house in Mill Valley, at the foot of quiet Mount Tam, back when hippies could still afford property in Marin County. Their music school had prospered with the region. Time and responsibility had blunted the edges of their radical views, but hadn't snuffed the old wild spark entirely. For as long as she could remember a cluster of handsome pot plants had grown in their back yard.

Art school had taken Nita over to the East Bay, where she was still living when she met Wright. To him, her parents' story was proof that the Bay Area was over—at least for a starting-out architect and an artist-turned-designer. What they'd done, you couldn't do now—not with all the tech moguls and investment bankers outbidding each other on properties and wrecking the market for everyone else. Charming place, the Bay Area, but that window was closed. Cleave Springs was still open.

Nita knew he was right, but that didn't make her first month in Cleave Springs any less lonely. It didn't stop her pining for the predictable summer weather of home. She was used to an arid climate, rain rarely falling between May and October. Here storms could crash through at any time. This bugged her, yet she was starting to like the liberties all that rain encouraged. As she and Wright stood in their yard now, her eyes passed with satisfaction over the deep-orange day lilies she'd planted in a side bed, the sedum and sweet woodruff she'd put in along the front walk, the hydrangeas whose round puffs of pink petals drew attention away from the wretched little house that had been cheap compared to Bay Area prices yet still a serious stretch for them.

Wright stood with his arm around her, wearing that professional gaze again, looking beyond her colorful plantings, past the actual house and into his preferred reality.

"Just wait," he said after a while, sliding behind her so he could reach forward and place both hands on her bulging womb.

"Until?"

He pulled her close, pressing his front tightly to her back and talking softly into the side of her neck. "You won't recognize it when I'm done."

THE FULL-SCALE RENOVATION Wright was planning would have to wait a couple of years. In the meantime, small projects scratched his itch to make something. The first thing he built was a waist-high wooden fence to keep their child safely in the front yard. Never mind that the child wasn't born yet.

While working on his fence one evening halfway through the second month, he struck up a conversation with Hannah and Jen. Wright and Nita got into the habit of chatting with Hannah and Jen as they walked back home from the right of way playground, where they brought their one-year-old, Jordan, to swing almost every evening. Hannah was a massage therapist, Jen an FBI agent who specialized in gang crimes.

Jen's law-and-order manner put Nita off at first. But she was rich in neighborhood information and generous with what she'd gathered. One evening, after Ash moped by on the sidewalk across the street, Nita asked Jen if she knew his story. Jen confirmed that Ash lived in the second-floor apartment of the sad building next door. The hard-drinking man in the painting clothes was the boyfriend of Ash's mother. The mother, a junkie, never left the house. The boyfriend made enough money painting to keep himself supplied with beer and weed. The rest of the household income, such as it was, came from Ash's grandmother, who sent checks from somewhere out of state.

"Who takes care of Ash?" Nita asked.

"Kid takes care of himself, basically." Jen's voice ran as level as the hem of the brown bangs on her forehead.

"He doesn't seem to have any friends."

"Flies solo, pretty much."

The following Saturday, Wright and Nita had dinner at Hannah and Jen's house for the first time. A big summer storm had moved through the area the night before, pulling mild, dry air from Canada in behind it. Everyone in the neighborhood seemed to be outside celebrating the weather as Wright and Nita walked over to the 1920s bungalow Hannah and Jen had restored.

Wright was excited to see the house. Jen opened him a beer and poured Nita a glass of seltzer. Nita recognized the calico Hannah was holding—white with patches of orange and black. The cat looked heavier than she remembered. She reached out and stroked its head. "What happened to you, beautiful? You used to come by our house all the time."

"Athena stays inside now," Hannah said.

Jen held little Jordan on her hip while she gave Wright and Nita the tour. They had moved in eight years before and had done all of the indoor work first, putting a great deal of time and care into reversing decades of heavy-handed "improvements" and outright neglect, peeling back the layers, returning their Craftsman house to the simple beauty of its first days.

"Nice," Wright said, noting the choices they'd made. "Of course. Yes. Oh, hell yes."

"Why don't you put the goddess down and take this guy," Jen said to Hannah when the tour ended. "I'll show them around outside while you get Jordan ready for bed."

Jen had used her vacation time the year before to build a cedar deck off the back of the house. Nita stood by herself up on the deck as Jen led Wright down the sloping lawn to show him the shed she'd built a couple of years before. The deck was elevated such that Nita could see over the top of the back fence, which bordered on a dense stand of bamboo that grew not in someone else's back yard, she began to realize, but in the fenced-off section of the right of way. She hadn't guessed their lot backed up to this forbidden zone. The image of Ash standing inside the fence, milk jug in hand, finger on lips, flashed into her mind as goose bumps rose on her forearms.

They ate dinner on the deck. Nita set Little Hoover in motion with several bites of grilled chicken and Caesar salad before mentioning to the hosts that she and Wright were curious about the space behind their yard.

It had been fenced off for ten or twelve years, Jen told them. "You can't blame people for feeling vulnerable. Cleave Springs was different ten years ago. Houses got robbed all the time."

Wright made his case for reopening the right of way and running the bike path all the way from Brimslea to the highway.

"Nice idea," Jen said, "but some of the people back here won't go for it."

"The neighborhood's changing," Wright said.

"They're not so scared anymore. They just don't want to lose the space." She turned in her chair and pointed. "Guy over here grows vegetables in the section behind his yard. Another family put a swing set in there for the kids. Personally, I'd be happy if the city came in and chopped down the bamboo behind our lot. It's all I can do to keep that stuff from taking over my yard."

"The Moores haven't found Jasmine," Hannah said. She'd been quiet all through dinner. Now she was leaning back in her chair while Athena dozed in her lap.

Wright smiled. "The Moores?"

"They live up the street," Jen said. "Jasmine's their cat."

Hannah nodded. "They haven't seen her for two days."

"A few cats have gone missing lately," Jen said. "Which worries Hannah more than it does me. She's sweet on cats."

Wright frowned. "I'm allergic to them."

"Not me," Jen said. "I just don't like them. Ask the goddess."

Hannah lifted Athena and made a show of cuddling the cat close to her bosom. "You're hurting her feelings." Nita couldn't tell if Hannah's scowl was real or not.

"Poor thing," Jen said. "It's tough to be an indoor pussy."

"Fuck you, Jen." Hannah got up with the cat and went into the house.

Jen sighed loudly and folded her hands behind her head. "Crap."

Nita waited. When she was convinced Jen had no intention of going after Hannah, she pushed her plate away, hauled her body up out of the chair and went inside. The cat was curled up on an ottoman in the living room, but Nita didn't find Hannah until she checked the front porch. A wicker couch backed up to the front of the house. Hannah sat on it sniffling. Nita sat down next to her and took hold of her hand.

"I guess I wrecked the party," Hannah said.

Nita squeezed her hand. "Are you okay?"

"I just hate it when Jen pulls this kind of shit. As if we didn't all know she's the breadwinner."

Nita cried so often at this point in her pregnancy that she always had tissues on her. She pulled one from her pocket and dabbed at Hannah's face. "I'm sure you do plenty."

"Taking care of a child is hard work, Nita. Everyone tells you that, but you can't really know until you're doing it. While Jen's running around keeping riffraff off the streets of America, I'm with Jordan all damn day."

"She must know that's work."

Hannah nodded. "But her job is so stressful. It's scary, you know? How can being with a toddler and giving a few massages a week stack up against chasing thugs full-time?"

Nita imagined that Hannah gave very good massages. She was muscular through the arms and shoulders, strong enough to dig for the deep tissue. She carried herself with a kind of rooted grace. Her black hair was straight, her eyelashes long and thick. She smelled like vanilla. Nita let go of her hand and stroked her bare shoulder.

Hannah placed her hand over Nita's. "Jordan's been waking up in the night all week. We're wiped out right now. Jen keeps herself together no matter what, but I let things get to me. I haven't been a very good host."

"I've had a lovely evening," Nita said. They sat for a few minutes holding hands, their heads resting lightly against each other. Nita talked to her friends back home on the phone a lot, they emailed back and forth, but she missed the physical part of being with those women. Comforting Hannah comforted her as well.

She explained this to Wright in bed later, after he complained about being invited to a dinner party and having to witness a quarrel between the hosts. "I like Hannah and Jen," she said, "and I'm glad they felt free to have a spat in front of us."

"That was pretty nasty, what Jen said."

"Well, she's stressed out. They're both tired. Jordan's been up a lot at night lately."

The droning air conditioner was silent for once, the bedroom window open to the cool night. They lay side by side, dry air caressing their skin. He reached over and placed his open palm on her belly. "Little Hoover, are you going to run your mommy and daddy ragged too?"

"We'll be tested," Nita said.

"We're already *being* tested, aren't we?"

An important question—*the* important question—formed into words on this night when a little storm in their friends' house made Wright nervous about the weather at home. Nita waited. She wasn't going to give him an easy answer.

"It's not like you *chose* Cleave Springs," he said. "It's not like you had a job waiting for you here, or a really nice house to move into, or people you knew. Your parents are a long way away."

"They are."

He rose up on his elbow and looked into her face. "I know

it's a huge adjustment for you. There's no guarantee this'll work for us."

"But you want it to work so much, Wright. I've never seen you so excited."

"I *am* excited about the possibilities here. But it has to work for both of us, not just me. If it doesn't, we can leave." He gathered a corner of the sheet and dried her cheeks with it. "I'm serious, Nita. We don't have to stay."

She'd made love with some self-conscious men, partners who sought to please and perform, but she liked Wright's unaffected presence better. Without being told, he accepted that making love with a pregnant woman was an unpredictable venture, subject to the momentary needs and mysterious chemistry of a body not entirely itself. As they fell to kissing now, touching each other in this blessed bubble of Canadian air, his hands stroked her patiently as his body moved around hers in a careful, exploratory way, eventually discovering a path into her that hadn't existed yesterday and would probably be overgrown tomorrow.

Afterward he dropped quickly off to sleep while Nita luxuriated next to him, enjoying a contentment unlike anything she'd felt for months, Wright's words making her feel free to end this experiment, yet the whole evening leaving her more positive than she'd felt so far about making a life here.

A noise came through the open window. A shrill sound, a cry like the one she'd heard that evening weeks back when she and Wright had stood outside the locked gate in the right of way. The wail of a hurt child, maybe. Or a cat.

ON MONDAY, she made sure she was out in front of the house when Ash came off the school bus. She walked up the sidewalk to head him off before he could veer into the right of way.

"Ash, hello. I wonder if you could help me."

He waited.

"Wright says I'm not allowed to lift a shovel until after the baby comes. I wonder if you'd like to make some money digging a flower bed for me."

He glanced off in the direction of the right of way. "Now?" The voice's clean tone surprised her anew.

"Now would be best. Could you?"

He followed her across the street and into the back yard. She set him up with a shovel, showed him where to dig, and went into the house to get him a glass of water.

Ash was not lazy but he worked without any apparent connection to the task, handling the shovel like he'd never seen one before. While he whacked feebly at the ground, Nita walked around the yard with a big drawing pad, sketching her ideas for future plantings. Eventually she lost her patience and asked if she could borrow the shovel. She showed him how to place his foot on the butt end of it and concentrate his weight there, forcing the blade into the earth, then pushing down on the handle to turn and expose the soil. She was aware of his odor but not nearly as revolted by it as she had been two months before.

He made better progress after her demonstration. When he was more than half-finished, she went inside to find some cash and make sandwiches. She offered him a plate when the bed was all dug. They didn't have any outdoor furniture yet so she invited him to sit on the back steps. She kept her distance while he attacked the food, coming close only after he'd cleared the plate and wiped his face on his arms. She stood across from the steps where he sat. His eyes quickly zeroed in on the fist that held the bills.

"You spend a lot of time in the right of way." She pointed off in the direction of the fenced-off part and he turned his head that way a moment. "You must like it back there."

His chin dipped once, the slightest nod.

"I saw you in there one time. I think you saw me too." A bead of sweat trickled down her spine. "Was that a jug of milk you were holding?"

Another nod.

"What was the milk for? You put your finger to your lips when you saw me. Is it a secret?"

He looked at the ground.

"You know why I looked through the fence right then?" she said. "Because I heard something. Did you hear it?"

He started digging at his cuticles and she noticed how raw they were.

"Can you tell me what I heard?" she said, and waited a moment. "Was it a cat?"

He raised his eyes again and held her gaze briefly before looking away.

"You know why I guessed it was a cat, right?"

"The milk," he said.

"Listen, Ash, you've been really helpful to me and Wright.

We appreciate that. I'd like to help you if there's some way I can."
She heard Wright's car pull up in the driveway; her time was running out. "It would be easier for me to help you if I knew what happened to that cat."

He shook his head no.

"You won't tell me?"

"Can't."

"Why not?"

"Wouldn't do that."

"Do what?"

"Not to them."

"Them?"

Wright was whistling inside the house. Ash didn't seem to hear him yet. He kept at his cuticles. "They need her," he said.

"I'm not following you, Ash."

His eyes rose and met hers again, more boldly than before. The weight of his spirit lifted briefly, like a window-shade rising.

Wright called out: "You here, babe?"

She watched Ash's face crack a slight grin, dry lips parting to give her a glimpse of mossy teeth.

WRIGHT'S FIRM WAS COMPETING for a big museum commission and he buzzed about the concept nonstop as they made dinner and ate. He didn't get around to asking about her afternoon until they were finished. "How'd it go with Ash?" he said. "Looks like he dug a decent bed."

"After I showed him how to use a shovel. I don't think he'd ever dug with one before."

Wright shook his head, marveling. "He's a teenager, right?

How do you live that long and never use a shovel?"

"No one cared enough to teach him," Nita said, and that was all it took to bring the tears that had threatened to gush since the moment Ash had stuck her bills in his pocket and left. "Treat a child like that and what do you expect? You think he won't take revenge?"

"Whoa," Wright said, coming over to her side of the table. He sat down and put his arm around her. "Where are we going here?"

When she could talk, she told him everything—about the first noise, when she saw Ash with the jug of milk, about the disappearing cats, about late Saturday night when she heard that sound come through the open window.

"Is that why you hired him today?" Wright said. "You wanted to ask him about all this?"

"Does anyone ever just talk to the kid, listen to him? I doubt it."

"You've been keeping all this to yourself. How come you didn't say anything before now?"

"I wasn't even sure I heard something that first time. You were right next to me and you didn't hear it. The second time you were asleep."

"And when you talked to him today? Did he fess up?"

"Sort of. Not really."

"What did he say?"

"Well, he knew exactly what I was talking about. He didn't deny anything, but he didn't exactly take responsibility. He almost sounded like he was covering for someone."

"A friend?"

"I've never seen him go back there with anyone."

Wright knit his brows. "An imaginary friend?"

Nita shrugged.

"Weird," Wright said.

"What should we do?"

"Maybe we should get Jen's advice."

"I don't know," Nita said. "What if she sends the police to hassle Ash? Is that going to help him?"

"Look, if he's murdering people's cats he's got to be stopped. Then we can see about getting him some help."

Wright went into the kitchen and picked up the phone. Nita listened to him explaining the situation to Jen, the two of them bonding in defense of the animals they despised.

"The city police have an officer assigned to Cleave Springs," Wright said when he hung up. "She'll call him in the morning."

Nita's throat tightened. "That's right, send the cops after him."

"You have a better idea?"

"This whole thing just sickens me."

Wright nodded. "The kid *is* creepy."

"The situation, Wright, not the kid. You and Jen don't care about Ash. You don't care about the cats, either. You care about your precious neighborhood and what it's going to be like one day when every house is beautiful and the right of way is a sanitized bike path and junkie women and their alcoholic boyfriends and their freaky kids don't live next door. That's what you care about. And *that's* creepy."

She left the table and went to the bedroom. Pretty soon she

heard Wright clearing the dinner dishes. He was biding his time, waiting for her to calm down. Well, let him wait. She picked up the phone and called her parents' house, wanting to go for at least a little while where those voices could take her, back to the bosom of old Mount Tam.

But they weren't home. She opened a magazine and tried to find a comfortable position on the bed. She kept reading the same sentences over and over as she tracked Wright's movements around the house. After finishing in the kitchen, he gathered up all the trash and went outside to take the big green bin and the yellow recycling tub down to the curb. He came back in and things got very quiet, which could only mean one thing. Outraged, she hauled herself off the bed and went to the doorway of his study.

"You're working on your drawings?"

He looked up. "I know we're not through talking. It seemed like we could use a little more time to cool off."

"I don't want to cool off."

He pushed his glasses onto his forehead. "What do you want, Nita?"

"I want you to say what you said to me Saturday night."

"Saturday night?"

"When we came home from Jen and Hannah's and you started fishing for some reassurance from me about bringing us here."

"What I said about us staying, you mean?"

She nodded. "People say all kinds of things when they want to get laid."

"Come on, Nita. I meant what I said."

"Do you still mean it?"

"Two days have passed. Nothing's changed."

"For you, maybe."

He had been talking over his shoulder, but now he swiveled in the chair to face her. "What's going on, babe? Ash really got to you today, didn't he?"

"We're going to have a baby, Wright. You and me. Soon."

He rose from the chair and approached, putting his arms around her. "And we're going to make a nice home for it, and teach it how to use a shovel."

"Don't mock me," she said, pushing him away.

Confusion brought the smile to his face, not contempt, yet his expression still annoyed her. "Quit fucking smiling."

"Sorry," he said.

"You think Ash's mom *tried* to fail? You think she didn't plan to take care of him?"

"Nita," Wright said, "you're going to be a wonderful mother. I know it."

"And what if something happens to me?"

"I'll be here," he said, and studied her face a moment. "You doubt that?"

"There aren't any blueprints for raising a child, Wright. There isn't a code book you can memorize."

"I thought you wanted to do this with me."

His hurt tone told her she should reach out to him now, but she folded her arms over her belly instead. "It's just that Ash, a kid like him—that's what failure looks like. What it *smells* like."

"Ash. Why are you so interested in him all of a sudden?"

"It isn't sudden."

Wright nodded. "I saw how he disgusted you that first day. You couldn't even shake his hand. You barfed the minute he left the house."

"True."

"But now look. We're arguing about him like he's part of our life. Like he's not some random pathetic kid. Like he matters to us. Like he's, I don't know—*relevant*." He snatched the glasses off his forehead. "I came here to succeed, Nita, not to fail. Why did you come here?"

"Because I loved you."

"*Loved* me?"

"I did."

SHE SLEPT BADLY and woke up remorseful. All morning she imagined scenes that might be playing out in Ash's summer school classroom, every one of them featuring a broad-shouldered cop with a crew cut barging in and jerking Ash from his desk. But then she'd remind herself that disappearing cats were probably not the police department's top priority. She resolved to do her best to confess to Ash what she'd done as soon as possible, to warn him about what was coming and apologize in advance.

Wright called twice from the office, but she let him go to voicemail both times. It was too hot for her to putter in the front yard while she waited for the school bus. She stayed inside after lunch and kept a close eye on the clock. Ten minutes before the bus was due, the phone rang.

"Hi Hannah."

"Nita?" Panic roiled Hannah's voice.

"What's wrong?" Nita said.

"Nita, you have to help me. Athena got out."

"When?"

"A few minutes ago? I don't know. I'm so stupid. Jordan slid the back door open and I didn't notice until just now. Fuck. *Fuck.*"

"Listen to me, Hannah. We'll find her. Don't worry."

"I can't leave the house, Nita. Jordan's napping." She sobbed. "If something happens to Athena…"

"Calm down," Nita said. "You stay there and I'll find her for you. Any idea which way she went?"

"I didn't see her."

"The right of way, you think?"

"That's where she liked to go when I used to let her outside. Before all the…"

"Hannah, listen to me. You're going to stay there with Jordan, and I'm going to find Athena for you, and I'm going to bring her there. Okay?"

"Maybe you should stay with Jordan and I could go out." Hannah's voice sounded steadier.

"No."

"It's hot out there, Nita. You should be inside."

"No," Nita said more firmly, and Hannah didn't press.

She stepped out of her sandals, pulled on some socks and sturdy shoes, and went to the sink to fill a water bottle. Outside, she pressed her straw gardening hat onto her head and cut across the front yard to the embankment above the old rail bed. She

descended the little slope at an angle and walked along the edge
of the dog area until she reached the metal fence.

The gate swung back pretty easily when she pulled it. She
paused before the opening and exhaled loudly, like she'd learned
in birthing class. *I'm not following you,* she'd said to Ash yesterday,
and he'd cracked a grin.

The world beyond the fence was unlike anyplace she'd experienced before. Struggle and strife were everywhere, with
grasses and bushes and vines and trees all vying for limited sunlight and space. A well-worn path led her into this riot of growth,
then branched, and kept branching until she couldn't tell the side
paths from the main stem and had a hard time keeping track of
her general direction. Some of the shrubs and trees and grasses
she saw were natives, no doubt, old residents reclaiming habitat
wrested away by people long before. But Nita was a stranger here,
an exotic herself, with no way of knowing which plants had his-
toric claims and which were invaders. She did recognize some of
what she saw, trumpet creepers and wisteria and honeysuckle
vines that had escaped from back yards and claimed sections of
the right of way. Clumps of daylilies grew in a few spots, the last
of their orange blossoms spread to the sun. The bamboo grove
beyond Hannah and Jen's yard was not the only such stand.

Here and there the frenzy of warring plants was interrupted
by a square of managed ground where vegetables grew in neat
rows, by a swing set and sand box, even a tiny pond edged with
river rocks. In two spots, she discovered falling-down wooden
forts whose makers had moved on to other forms of play. As
she followed the winding paths, the ring of Hannah's panicked
voice diminished in her ears and the image of calico Athena

receded to the back of her mind. This feral space consumed her attention and occupied her senses. Shapes and colors clashed. Light shifted, scents collided. She wandered.

Yet as she wandered, dodging thorny briars, ducking vines, veering onto path after winding path, she sensed she was somehow progressing. So she was not exactly surprised when she reached the edge of a bright clearing and saw, across the heads of the tall grasses that grew there, the crisp profile of pointed ear and snout. Except for that ear and snout, and the bushy black tip of the tail, the animal was hidden in the grass. But she knew a coyote when she saw one. It stood no more than twenty yards from her, eyes and ears pointed forward, so locked in on the object of their attention that the coyote was oblivious to Nita's arrival. Nita shifted her gaze right, following the coyote's line of sight until her own eyes came to rest on Athena. The cat crouched on the far side of the clearing, lapping hungrily at one of several silver bowls.

One word from Nita—a sudden movement—would have saved the cat. But Athena was not the one she had come here to protect.

Drunk on free milk, her instincts dulled by too many nights in the bungalow, Athena never even sensed the attack coming. A short yowl of surprise, a scream of panic, and she was silent.

The coyote carried the dead cat by the throat, trotting light-footed back across the clearing until a breeze came up and advertised Nita's presence. The coyote stopped, glanced right at Nita, fixing her with a pair of sober, appraising eyes, then turned and bounded off into the high grass.

"Ash," Nita said loudly, "are you here?" She looked all around the clearing. "Come out."

A jay shrieked behind her. She pulled out her water bottle and took a long drink, her eyes on the clearing. The boy emerged from the mouth of a little trail to her left.

"Where does it take the cats?" Nita said.

He led her across the clearing toward where the coyote had disappeared. Soon they were deep into the right of way's network of paths, Ash guiding her swiftly from path to path, proprietary, confident, a master of this strange geography. Walls of vegetation cut off the view to either side, but she began to hear traffic up ahead. Eventually they emerged at the top of a steep, grassy embankment, at the edge of which stood a metal fence. The highway was just across the fence. Beyond the highway stretched a swath of open land, site of the long-defunct railyard where, Wright had told her, every man in Cleave Springs once worked. Construction crews had recently broken ground for the vast box mall that would fill that acreage.

Ash pointed down to the bottom of the embankment, toward the dark round opening of a culvert. "She goes through that pipe to get across the highway. After that, she sneaks across that whole big job site. Her den is by the river. She's got seven pups."

Nita never suspected Ash could string so many words together. "How do you know?"

"I followed her. A few times."

The smell rising from the culvert, all too familiar, quelled any doubts she might have about this claim.

"How'd a coyote get here?"

He grinned.

"I mean, I thought they only lived out West. *Jesus*," she marveled, a classroom map of North America unfurling before her mind's eye, scores of blue waterways spilling to either side of the Continental Divide and webbing the continent's body like veins. The muscular Rockies ran from top to bottom, cleanly dividing West and East. The whole picture seemed temporary now, negotiable. "What's *that* about?"

"Wolves lived here before people killed them off. A teacher said that."

The boy had actually learned something in school. The possibility had never occurred to her.

"So," she said, "there was an opening."

They turned together, but she wasn't ready to start back. "Ash, did you buy milk with the money Wright and I paid you?"

"And bowls."

"Why do you do it?" she said. "Why do help her catch the cats?"

"Not for her."

They need her, he had told her yesterday. "Oh, for the pups."

It pleased him, she saw, that he didn't have to spell this out to her. He pointed toward her belly. "Got a name yet?"

"It's funny, Ash. I have this feeling that when I see the child, I'll know."

"Manzanita," he said.

"A wild queen of a plant, my dad always told me, beautiful and tough."

He lingered, kicking at the ground.

"Ash is such an interesting name," she said. "Do you know how your parents chose it?"

"I didn't know ash was a kind of tree until Wright said it. I went home and asked my mom if that's where my dad and her got my name." He looked over toward the culvert.

"What did she say?"

"She couldn't remember."

"Oh, Ash." Nita stepped up and embraced the boy. She breathed in his atmosphere, stewing in the fearful odors of neglect as her hands clasped tightly on his ribby back.

Before they headed for home, Nita explained what was going to happen next. The police would come to question him about the disappearing cats, and he would swear he knew nothing about it. He would stay out of the right of way for at least the next two months. He would tell no one about the coyote, and she would also keep quiet about that. Together, they would figure out a safer way to keep the pups from going hungry.

They were quiet as he led her back through the bushy labyrinth, across the same ground where on nice days, a few years deeper in, she would ride her bike along a sinuous asphalt path through expanses of clipped green lawn, her little girls chattering in the trailer behind the bike, their names as much a part of them as the whorled patterns on their fingertips. Even then, her own house transformed into two stories of grace and light, the apartment house next door renovated and rented out to tenants of a different kind, Nita would never travel this section of the right of way without stopping briefly to free the girls from the trailer and lead them in a chorus of howls.

WONDERS OF THE WORLD

U P SIX RUNGS of the step ladder, through the square portal of the attic hatch, and the top half of me entered another realm.

Zach crouched a few feet away, gloved hands on a half-unrolled coil of insulation, eyes scolding me above a surgical mask. The attic air had a bit of body to it, like a thin wine. Thin and acrid. Each breath brought more microscopic fibers to the back of my throat. I pirouetted slowly, surveying all I could with the aid of the single spotlight Zach had clamped to a rafter, my careful toes working their way around the surface of the rung.

When I completed the circle Zach pulled down the mask. He pointed at the hatch. "Down. Right now."

I cleared my throat to dislodge tiny fibers and pointed toward something I'd noticed—a dim glow toward the front of the house. "What's that?"

Zach cleared his throat—to dislodge *me*.

"At least I notice things," I said.

"What didn't I notice?"

"You didn't even see that little glow over there, did you?"

Zach sighed. A distance runner, he has capacious lungs.

"Three years, and we're just now insulating this attic," he finally said. "Three years of money flying out through the roof. I was focusing on this job."

"Mr. Focus."

"What's that supposed to mean?"

Some couples keep things lively by having sex in unusual places. For Zach and me, it was kind of nice to bicker someplace new.

"Do you really want to know?" I said.

Evidently not. He pulled the mask up over mouth and nose and turned toward the front wall of the house. He shuffled along on hands and knees, following a pair of joists like train tracks, his caboose receding in the gloom. Before long he reappeared, face first. The object in his right hand caught the light briefly on each forward shuffle. Near the edge of the hatch he shifted positions and handed the object to me, lowering the mask.

"Your glow."

An empty can. A steel can, judging from the weight. I studied it in the light that rose through the hatch. The side bore an image of a woman holding scales in one hand and a sword in the other. A blindfold covered her eyes. Bare feet showed beneath the hem of her flowing robe. Beneath her feet, forming a kind of pedestal to support her, the words **JUSTICE LAGER**. Banners flared up diagonally from either side of the pedestal. Inside these were the words *Tastes Right*.

"It's old," I said.

"One of the original builders must have left it behind. 1936, this house was built."

"1936," I mused. "Hoover Dam completed."

"Here we go," Zach said.

"Four million, three-hundred-sixty-thousand cubic yards of concrete in that dam. And get this: a total of twenty-one-thousand men worked on the project."

"That's a lot of workers," he said. "I'm glad somebody was free to build this fine little duplex in Cleave Springs."

"Free and thirsty."

"And careless with our ship."

"Our ship?"

He reached over and took the can from me, raised it up and inspected it. "The one that just came in."

THAT EVENING, after Ruth fell asleep, we placed a sheet-covered box on the center of the dining room table and staged a photoshoot. We captured the can from every possible angle, handling it with great care during each change of pose.

"Why is Justice a woman?" Zach asked.

"It started with the Greeks. Themis was their goddess of justice and law. Justicia was one of the four virtues for the Romans."

"Why not have a god of justice and law?"

"Well, women are more merciful," I said.

"Is that why she's holding a sword?"

"The sword is a symbol of power."

He leaned his slender trunk forward over the table and studied the image closely. "And the symbol for mercy?"

"I suppose that's implied."

"By what? All I see is a sword for power, scales for fairness, and a blindfold for…" He turned. "Excuse me, the woman is holding a sword and wearing a blindfold?"

"Most people say the blindfold's another symbol for fairness. You know, to be totally impartial, justice has to be blind to the individuals involved in a case. Others say the blindfold's ironic, some jilted sculptor's complaint about the fairness of the courts. She didn't start wearing the blindfold until the 16th century."

We waited for his sigh to end.

"All right," he said, "the Greek and Roman thing, I believe you knew that already. But the 16th century sculptors? Please tell me you went online."

"I learned about the blindfold the summer after 10th grade. Family trip to Washington. We took a tour of the Supreme Court."

"And you still remember about the 16th century sculptors? That's sick."

"And *that's* thoughtful," I said, but cut him off before he could retract. "What I'd really like to know about is Justice Lager. You know, what's the history there?"

"I'm sure the high bidder can fill you in."

"Don't you think we should know what we've got here, before we start the auction?"

Zach reached over to stand the can upright. "What we've got here could be a very nice little piece of windfall. Another couple might be sentimental, put it up on a shelf and trot it out at dinner parties to start conversation. What this couple needs to do is convert it into cash."

❖ ❖ ❖

ZACH WAS ALREADY a devoted runner when we met. When Ruth was born, he started competing in ultra marathons, road races that stretch 50, 75, 100 miles—sometimes even longer. Between races, he trains fanatically, which doesn't leave him much time for making money. He actually finished law school a few years ago, but you can't work for a law firm and be a serious ultra marathoner. He works odd hours in our garage, building and fixing bikes for people who ride the same way he runs.

In former times we could have afforded to be sentimental about Dame Justice. When we got together, I was a senior researcher at Wonders of the World Channel. The money was fairly good. For several years we stayed in his cheap one-bedroom place at the Dogwood, a skanky apartment complex beside a strip mall. We called it the Dogfart. The picture window in our unit looked out over the dumpster and grease barrels behind an International House of Pancakes. The apartment's onion-skin walls couldn't begin to shield us from the nocturnal noises of Tammy, the next door tenant, whose sexual stars typically aligned between four and five in the morning.

By enduring these and other hardships, Zach and I saved half of my salary every month. We used most of that nest-egg for the down payment on our house. The leftover savings bought me six months of maternity leave after Ruth was born. Near the end of those six months I experienced a bout of blindness, which delayed my return to work. My vision came back after a few days, but then flickered out again for a while. That turned the delay into a holding pattern. Maternity leave was replaced by sick leave, which gave way to resignation. Disability checks were smaller than the paychecks they replaced, and the due date of each month's mortgage payment was now a black spot on our calendar.

ZACH LIKES TO START TRAINING around the same time neighbor-Tammy used to shout for the deity. The morning after the photo shoot, he left the house well before dawn. Audrey was already in the kitchen when Ruth and I came downstairs, both of us still in our PJs.

"Good morning, girls," Zach's mother sang out to us. She stood framed by the kitchen door, trim in her burgundy velour warm-ups.

"Grammy!" Ruth ran to Audrey, who bent to scoop my girl up in her arms.

"Guess what Grammy's wearing this morning?"

"Soft suit!" Ruth pulled the hood to the front of Audrey's shoulder and rubbed her cheek avidly on the velour.

"Guess what Grammy made you for breakfast?" She set Ruth down in front of a bowl of oatmeal. "I would have made some for Mama, too."

"No," Ruth said sternly, "Mama cave."

I turned toward the stairs. "Mama's going up to get her breakfast."

Our house was designed as an over-under duplex; we live on both floors. We originally planned to convert the upstairs kitchen into a walk-in closet, but my fickle vision upstaged that project before Zach ever lifted a hammer. The specialists ran me through a battery of tests, and they concluded that those two episodes of blindness signaled a breach in the integrity of my central nervous system. No one could predict exactly where it would go from there. What I have comes at you in waves. The interval between waves, the size and shape of the trough, is different for each person. Like waves, it can't be denied—only resisted. My resistance strategy yokes the old to the new. I swallow pills with unpronounceable names and eat food from the Stone Age. The Paleolithic Diet, gurus call it. Zach calls my kitchen the Cave.

Breakfast this morning was elk jerky with raw walnuts and dried blueberries on the side. When I descended the stairs with my plate of delicacies I found Ruth sitting bibbed and boostered at the table, hard at work on an oatmeal mask. Audrey stood near the window holding the Justice Lager can aloft; she swallowed the end of a Jesus song and showed me an apologetic smile.

"How *are* you today?"

"Well, my eyes worked when I opened them this morning. That's always encouraging. Looks like I can still conquer the stairs." I sat down next to Ruth. "What do you think of Dame Justice?"

"The can?" Audrey said. "It's neat. What a find."

I put some blueberries in Ruth's oatmeal bowl, then bit off a small piece of jerky and began to chew.

"What happens now?" Audrey said, as if Zach hadn't told her during last night's session on the phone.

"Zach wants to auction it off. I'd like to at least find out how rare it is first. What do you think?"

"Oh, I don't know anything about old beer cans."

"That's not what I meant. Do you think I should start the auction first thing this morning?"

"It's not up to me, is it?"

"The can belongs to you too."

She set it down. "How's that?"

She could pretend not to understand, but I wasn't fooled. The woman was not dull—just startled by the slightest glint of my sword.

"You've paid as much of the mortgage as we have the last six months."

"Just helping you two get back on your feet."

"Zach is on his feet—for about 200 miles a week. I'm just thankful I can see mine."

She zipped the warm-up jacket up over her breasts and folded her arms.

"I doubt you can afford to help us much longer," I said.

"Not financially, no."

"I figured we'd scraped the bottom of your bank account. Why else would Zach be panicking?"

"He's panicking?"

"The check is due in a week, he goes out and puts all that insulation on the credit card?"

Her brow wrinkled. "But insulation pays for itself."

"Over time, sure. And while the insulation's paying for itself, who the hell is paying the mortgage?" I tore the piece of jerky in two. "No wonder he's so hot to sell that can. If somebody buys it, he can keep ignoring what we've done to you."

Being bankrupted by her son bothered Audrey far less than

listening to me slander him. Her eyes fled mine and settled on Ruth. "Oh, love," she said, "did you miss your mouth?"

Ruth had a glob of oatmeal on one of her ears. No surprise there—those little ears act like vacuums, sucking the world to them. After kissing Ruth goodnight, I stand outside the bedroom door sometimes and listen as she combs back through the flotsam and jetsam that's washed up on the shore of her day. She sings snatches of Audrey's vile songs—"Jesus loves me this I know…"—and chants lines from books she likes—"Jeep goes beep. Jeep goes thud. Jeep goes deep in gooey mud." The skein of words usually features one or two that have surfaced in an adult conversation. *Litmus*, I once heard her say. Also *carbon* and *warranty*. Tonight, *mortgage* might make an appearance.

"Grammy!" Ruth shouted now. "Twirl me."

Audrey twirled away from her difficult daughter-in-law and glided over to Ruth, lifting my girl's chunky body up and into the kitchen. "First we wash, *then* we twirl."

Lesion. That was another word that once escaped Ruth's mouth as she talked herself up over the ridge and down into the valley of dreams.

I SPENT ALL OF EVERY DAY with Ruth throughout her first year. But as she got heavier, my muscles started going slack. A walk to the park became a workout. Lifting her to my hip got hard. When I started to need naps more than Ruth did, Audrey stepped into the breach. She and Zach's father split up twenty years ago. Since then, she's scratched out a living taking care of people's kids. When Zach asked if she could spend mornings with Ruth, she found a family who needed her in the afternoons and gave us the first half of every weekday.

I still spend afternoons and evenings with Ruth, but morning is my solo time: for rest, for exercise, and for research—today's top priority. If I started the auction cold, without learning a little about can collecting, bidders would know me for the ignoramus that I actually was.

I first went online and found my way to a website called Cantastic, a rich trove of beer can lingo and lore. Our 1936 Justice Lager can, I learned, dated back to the dawn of the beer can era. Until 1935, people who slurped beer at home slurped it only from bottles. Some of the early cans, including ours, had a cone-shaped top fashioned like a bottle's mouth to mollify people with reactionary lips. Collectors grade beer cans on a scale of 1 to 5, where 1 is like new and 5 is so damaged you can hardly recognize the brand. Mint is the category for a can like ours, so clean that 1 doesn't quite convey their purity. Most old cans, discovered in musty basements or "dumped" by can nuts from backwoods trash heaps, carry rust, dents, and scratches. Dame Justice had spent seven decades in a dry attic, a story removed from the rough and tumble of domestic life, resting safe from the ravages of rust and the gentle entropy of fade.

But was she rare? There were hundreds of beer cans up for sale on the auction site, but not a single Justice Lager can. A good sign, but it didn't really prove anything. Dame Justice might still be as common as a crow. The only way to know for sure was to search the pages of *United States Beer Cans*, the definitive reference source. Problem: the local library didn't own the book. Across the river, on the shelves of the Library of Congress, stood every book in print; but getting there involved a journey that would ruin me for the rest of the day. The publisher charged eighty dollars for the title, a bigger hit than the family purse could handle. Was there another way?

That night, in bed, Zach insisted that there was.

"The auction," he said, looking up from his running magazine. "Start the bidding and see where it goes. Have faith in the market."

"Faith is your thing. Yours and Audrey's."

He pretended deep interest in his magazine as I studied his bare torso. Zach has always been lean; ultra-marathoning has wizened him into a walking sinew. Pluck him and he'd probably produce a note.

"What are you reading?" I asked.

"New recipe for power bars."

If my kitchen is a cave, his is a lab. He's always in there with his mysterious jars, his scale and measuring spoons, trying to concoct the perfect portable food.

"Zachary," I said, "we can't suck your mother's tit forever."

He dropped the magazine across his chest.

"Her savings have dried up."

"Look," he said, "the Blue Ridge Challenge is almost here. If I win it, I should get a sponsor."

"Tell me something, Zach. How many ultra marathons have you won?"

"Well, I came in fourth in Rhode Island."

"And you're faster now than you were in Rhode Island six months ago?"

"Thanks for the support," he said.

"Okay, so let's suppose you are faster, or the other guys are slower. You win the Blue Ridge. You get a sponsor. You're not exactly competing in a marquee sport. What does a sponsor supply, shoe laces?"

"What if she didn't have to pay rent?" he asked.

"What if she lived here, you mean?"

"We have an extra room."

"Jesus songs," I said. "Day and night."

"Do you really think it'll damage the kid? She sang them when I was a child and I turned out okay, didn't I?"

"You're turning out a bit monkish, actually."

I reached under the covers. His thigh tensed when I touched it, but I didn't pull away. My fingers rested near his crotch.

"Look," he said, "you know how I get when I train."

"You've been training ever since I've known you. Not like this."

"It's the ultras—they're more demanding."

"And I'm less?"

I watched his face as he rehearsed answers, none of which he spoke.

"You scold me for climbing a ladder," I said, "but what would you lose if I fell and got hurt?"

He sighed. "Please. You know how important this is to me."

"I know a lot of things. I actually prefer knowledge to faith."

He removed my hand from his thigh and rolled over on his side, showing me his bony back. "Knowledge won't make us any money off that can."

❖ ❖ ❖

I LAUNCHED THE AUCTION the next morning. Within minutes, re-
morse began to gnaw. Dame Justice sat above the desk, on a shelf
next to my monitor—an enigma, a cipher. I hadn't even begun
to solve her. How could I just sell her off to some stranger?

I spent what remained of the morning at the Cantastic site,
reading the little essays the host wrote for his Can of the Month
section. This guy described himself as a professional historian
and he did display some skill at tracking down and arranging per-
tinent facts. Each of his essays gave the history behind one of
the cans in his vast collection.

Just before lunch, I mustered up the courage to send an email
to the address that appeared on the contact information page—
rusty@cantastic.com.

dear rusty, I wrote, what can you tell me about
justice lager? I signed it "thirsty."

I didn't get back to my computer until that night, just before
going to bed. First I checked the auction site. Dame Justice had
attracted some attention. Somebody who called himself Dump-
Daddy had gotten the ball rolling with a substantial bid. In re-
sponse, a candawg had bid enough money to buy a copy of
United States Beer Cans for everyone in my house.

I opened up my email and found a reply from Rusty: Hi
thirsty: what don't you know about justice
lager?

my can is empty, I wrote, and then shut down for the
night.

In the morning, I opened email first. Rusty had already writ-

ten back: do you have a justice lager can or are
you just being clever?

not just being clever, I replied.

While waiting for his answer I took Dame Justice down from
the shelf and fawned over her a bit. For the first time I noticed
that she had a blemish, a black spot shaped like a kidney bean
on the upper part of the arm that held the sword. Was this part
of the picture, or some small corruption on the surface of the
can? Rusty's reply landed before I could decide.

procedural matter, he wrote. i.m. would make
this easier.

His instant messenger screen name was "rusty"; mine,
"ruthsmom." agreed, I typed, and sent the message—my sex
no longer a secret.

Within seconds, he replied: what do you want to know
about the justice can? usbc already told you
how rare it is.

It took me a minute to figure out that USBC stood for *United
States Beer Cans.*

i want to know why, I wrote.

i appreciate that, thirsty.

we historians have to stick together.

right, Rusty answered. so why don't you tell me
what game you're playing.

not sure, I wrote.

hmm. what grade is your justice lager can?

does it matter?

just making sure it's the same one i see on
my screen.

on your screen?

you know, the one that triggered this bidding war.

I opened up the auction site and couldn't quite believe what
I saw. Late the previous evening, after I had checked out for the
night, a character called misterconetop had posted a gaudy bid.
You could practically hear him laughing at candawg and Dump-
Daddy. But my hat went off to candawg. After midnight, he laid
down a counterbid that showed misterconetop he wasn't going
to win Dame Justice without a fight. The two of them had
slugged it out all through the night. By now the can was worth
more than I paid for my first car.

so, I wrote to Rusty, i'm selling the can. can't
i be curious about it too?

usbc didn't tell you enough?

i don't own usbc. can't afford a copy.
won't need it after I sell the can.

thirsty and poor. and not into cans.

just interested in THIS can (which I found
in my attic). and history.

in that case, you found the right can.

a lot of history in this can?

if that can could talk...

I stood up, my heart thumping, beads of perspiration rising
along my hairline. "What game *am* I playing?" I said aloud. And
sat back down.

maybe *we* could, I wrote.

talk?

unless you want to write down what you
know.

it's better to see it with your own eyes.

see what?

history.

you'll send me pictures?

how about a tour?

I stood up again, hurried to the window, and looked outside.
I left my office and headed for the front door of the house, making sure it was locked before I returned to my keyboard.

damn it, rusty, don't tell me you know where
i live.

just guessing. if you found a justice lager
can in your attic, that means we're probably
neighbors. mid-atlantic region, right? justice
was a baltimore beer.

ok. mid-atlantic it is. now what?

i show you some relevant sites, if you want
to see them.

a field trip?

you game?

suspicious, I admitted.

you're right to be. what if we met somewhere safe, a public place?

in baltimore?

i'm actually closer to d.c.

me too.

hmmm, Rusty wrote, ever go to the main reading
room at the library of congress?

Gooseflesh rose on my arms. one of my favorite
places in the world.

mine too. the library of last resort.

NORMALLY I SHOWER AT NIGHT, before I go to bed, but the following morning I showered just after breakfast. Which made
Ruth curious.

"Where you going?" she kept asking as she watched me in
the shower. Her face filled a little gap between the shower curtain
and the wall.

"Mama has to run some errands," I kept answering.

Audrey tried to lure Ruth away with toys and books, but she
stayed underfoot as I dried off and got dressed.

"Where you going? Where you going, Mama?"

While I pulled on my linen slacks and blouse, she made a
couple of game attempts at walking in my pumps. She forgot all
about the shoes when I took the bottle of Obsession down off
the shelf and began dabbing it behind my ears.

"Hold that!"

I gave her the bottle, sure I'd secured the lid, but by the time
the shoes were on my feet she was pouring perfume on her head.
"Damn you!" I said, and pulled a lock of her hair as I was wrest-
ing the bottle away. She howled. Audrey appeared in the bedroom
doorway, standing back as if my caustic behavior might splash
up in her face.

"I'm leaving," I announced. "I'm going to be late."

"Well," she said quietly, "you look very nice."

The day was bright, a feel of fall in the air, yet the trees held fast to their green. Dame Justice rode in my handbag, swaddled in tissue paper, as I clacked toward the Cleave Springs Metro station. I didn't like leaving Ruth in distress, but as I rounded the first corner I started liking how it felt to be out of the house in the morning, put together and going somewhere with a definite purpose—like I was commuting to Wonders of the World Channel again. But I had never once worn Obsession to work. What game was I playing?

On the train, I rode with my bag on my lap, my arms folded over the top for extra security. Carrying a million-dollar diamond could not have made me more wary. A diamond might be worth more, but its surface is hard—invincible. Rough contact might scratch or dent Dame Justice.

The train passed through a few dim stations, then emerged into daylight as it approached the Potomac. The tide was in, the water high on the banks, a light wind wrinkling the river's surface. Up ahead, across the river, Rusty waited for me under the great dome of the Library of Congress reading room. He'd said I would know him by his I'D RATHER BE DUMPING T-shirt. Beyond the shirt, and a vague outline of a guy roaming the woods with a metal detector in one hand and a hoe in the other, I had no mental picture of the man. Yet I felt I already knew him. His words had created an impression. Not just through our online exchange, but also through the little essays he'd written for the Can of the Month section of his web site. By now I had read a couple of years' worth of these tasty pieces.

The typical Can of the Month essay featured a picture of a can from Rusty's collection, followed by an archival photo or two of the massive brick brewery that produced the beer. Rusty also tracked down advertisements from old newspapers and snapshots of billboards, signs, and labels. He usually included black-and-white portraits of legendary brewmasters as well, Old World men with stern eyes and prodigious beards. Rusty's words sketched in the human stories that swarmed around every brand of beer. As owners came and went, as families clashed and divided, as economies waxed and waned, as cities died off and grew, beer flowed. New brands, new labels, new varieties of beer were invented—sometimes *re*-invented—to keep pace with changing times and tastes. Beer was a commodity, a product in the marketplace, yet it was also a round stool in the corner bar with buddies after a hard day at the plant. It was out back with all the uncles and aunts, Saturday afternoon with meat on the grill and a ballgame on the radio. Beer was a label to know, a taste to share, a slogan that jingled in the ears of a whole city and the countryside around it. Beer was community in a can.

The promise of lessons that lay ahead helped me slog forward along a Capitol Hill sidewalk, closing in on the Library. My legs had weakened since I'd last worn pumps. Still, I would arrive on schedule, twenty minutes before the time Rusty and I had agreed to meet. I would pass through security, scout out a good spot in the reading room, and watch the entrance until he arrived. If I didn't like the look of him, I could slip away unnoticed. I'd given him no clues about my appearance.

Does anything ever go according to plan? As I walked toward the desk at the center of the circular room, a large man in a moss-colored flannel shirt approached me from the side.

"Thirsty?"

I stopped and faced him. He drew back the two halves of his unbuttoned flannel shirt, revealing a black T-shirt with white block lettering that announced what he'd rather be doing.

"You knew me," I said in a library voice.

His face, fair and round, flushed from the hairline down to the floor of the ample second chin. "You're carrying that bag like it's full of finch eggs."

"I just don't want anything to happen to her."

His frown was friendly. "Well, me either."

The room was as exhilarating as I remembered it—a grand temple of knowledge. The octagonal base, faced in earth-toned marble, supported a series of stacked arches. Above the arches rose the glorious dome. Bronze statues of great thinkers, artists, and explorers perched godlike in the highest arches while mortals sat far below at curved wooden tables, reading by the light of hooded lamps.

"Is this where you hang out?" I asked.

"Well, I'm comfortable working here."

"I've always liked it here too."

"You mentioned you were a historian."

"A pretty lazy one, yeah. I could have come over here to check out a copy of *United States Beer Cans*. Instead I started pumping you for information."

He pivoted and began walking—daintily for a man of his girth. Black canvas sneakers showed beneath his tan pants. I followed him along the curving outer edge of one of the tables that formed concentric rings in the great room. We soon arrived at his carrel, where books, folders, and a laptop lay neatly arranged beneath the brass lamp. He motioned for me to sit in the chair next to his.

"Here's a bit of the Justice Lager stuff," he said, lifting the cover of the top manila folder. "These came out of several boxes that live in my basement." He slid the folder in front of me. "Please, touch."

I began leafing through old photographs, newspaper advertisements and articles, copies of official-looking papers. A beer called Charm City was the subject of nearly every artifact. Rusty calmly recited the name of every person in every photograph. Three names—Old Wilhelm, Peter, and Karl—predominated.

"Several boxes?" I said when I reached the bottom of the folder. "Do you dig this deep on every project?"

"You might be interested to know that my surname is Rechter."

"Same as the guys in these pictures?"

He nodded. "Justice Lager is personal."

"But everything in here is about this Charm City beer," I said.

"Are you game for an excursion?" He flushed again, less deeply.

"To Baltimore?"

"Charm City," he nodded. "I brought my car."

To Baltimore and back was two hours of driving, and Rusty's tour would take time also. No way could I get home in time to relieve Audrey. If I went, Zach would have to let his wrenches rest and cover for me. And what about Rusty? Could I trust him to take me on an excursion? It was hard to imagine a less menacing man than this can-collecting historian. Was it his stack of folders? His dorky T-shirt? His mincing walk and barometric skin? Or was it me? For nearly two years, my body had been losing a battle of attrition. I already knew my nemesis; I lived with it every day. An onslaught by a predatory male seemed surreal to me, irrelevant, a horror from someone else's life.

"You'll tell me all about Justice Lager on the way?"

He opened a second folder and removed several typed, stapled pages. "I'll drive while you read."

THE JUSTICE LAGER CAN I carried in my handbag had once contained a beer sold for decades before Prohibition under the brand name Charm City Lager. Charm City was created by brewmaster Wilhelm Rechter, "Old Wilhelm," who emigrated to the United States from a village outside Munich in 1881.

Charm City struggled through the Prohibition years by making "near beer" and soda pop. Old Wilhelm died in 1929. At the end of Prohibition, in 1933, his adult sons, Peter and Karl, sought to revive the family business by making proper beer again. Peter proposed that the brewery change its traditional lager recipe by adding corn and rice and reducing the amount of barley. These cheap fillers would lighten the beer's flavor and lower production costs. Peter predicted the shift toward the lighter-bodied beers that would come to dominate the American market.

Brother Karl wanted nothing to do with this new recipe, which he considered a corruption. The Rechter brothers dissolved their partnership. Peter retained the Charm City brand name and began brewing his new beer a couple of miles away from the family's original brewery, where Karl made beer using the old recipe. Karl's beer was sold under the new brand name of Justice Lager.

Justice Lager sold poorly. In less than three years, Karl Rechter went bankrupt and Justice Lager ceased to exist. Meanwhile, Charm City prospered, reclaiming its status as the beloved "official" beer of Baltimore. Rusty's essay claimed the Justice Lager cone top was one of six or seven cans to merit the highest number, a perfect 10, on the rareness scale first proposed by Selleck and later refined by Stayman. Only a handful of Justice Lager cans were known to exist in collections worldwide.

FINISHED READING, I gazed out the car window for a while, letting the story settle into my mind. Trees lined both shoulders of the Baltimore-Washington Parkway, their leaves the dull green of late summer.

"Justice Lager," I said. "Why did Karl call it that?"

"A family thing."

"Doing justice to his father's recipe?"

"That, yes. Karl was a moralist. Plus, he was clever. *Sprechen Sie Deutsch?*"

"*Nein.*"

Rusty frowned goodnaturedly. "Well, in German, the word for 'right' is '*recht.*'"

"Oh," I said, "so Justice Lager is Rechter's beer. It tastes right."

"Well put."

"Why didn't his beer sell?" I said.

"Couldn't have been the taste. Karl was meticulous. He followed the old Charm City recipe to the letter. He watched over the brewing like a hawk. A lot of what made the distinctive Justice Lager flavor was the strain of yeast that Old Wilhelm had brought with him from Germany. Karl worshiped the Rechter yeast like a holy relic. He kept the strain pure all through Prohibition. He was brewing a quality beer."

"And Charm City did well, even though Peter fiddled with the recipe?"

"He didn't fiddle with the recipe. He tossed the recipe out the window and started brewing cheap swill. But did people notice? Did they care? They'd been through thirteen years of Prohibition. They remembered the name Charm City, they believed in the brand."

"Ah, belief," I said, the contempt in my voice answering the hint of scorn I'd heard in Rusty's.

He hunched forward over the wheel, his moss-colored back and shoulders like a turtle's domed shell.

"Rusty," I said after a minute, "are you going to tell me where we're headed?"

"Wishbone. It's a neighborhood—a part of town, at least."

As we approached Baltimore, I grew nostalgic about my favorite era at Wonders of the World Channel. I was in charge of research for a documentary series on great public works projects—dams, bridges, tunnels, and the like. I had learned an immense amount about the Fort McHenry Tunnel that takes cars under Baltimore's Inner Harbor. Riding along, I explained the immersed tube method of tunnel construction, quoted exact numbers for the length and width, construction dates, materials used, people employed, and so forth, trying to wow a fellow historian with what I knew.

Rusty pushed himself away from the wheel and settled against the backrest, his color rising again. "Ever read about what they found when they started the dredging for that project?"

"Not that I remember. What was it? Something gruesome?"

He nodded.

"What? A body?"

"Part of one."

I was still waiting for him to elaborate when we exited the freeway and plunged into the bleak outskirts of the city. Everything outside my windows—salvage yards, tow lots, razor-wire fences, buckled sidewalks, rotting houses, trashed furniture lining the roadsides—encouraged me to lock the doors. Yet inside, an air of calm prevailed. Rusty seemed oblivious to possible danger. After several desolate miles we came to a rust-bitten bridge that carried us across a narrow canal containing a liquid that looked like brake fluid. Things changed as soon we reached the other side of the canal. A cheerful orange awning was the first feature to catch my eye. The awning sloped away from the sheer face of a building approximately a dozen stories high, an old brick industrial structure with new windows; a recent sandblasting had brought a soft, peachy color out of the aged bricks. On the sidewalk beneath the awning, people sat at café tables. Rusty pulled over to the side of the street in front of a florist's shop. He pointed toward the building with the orange awning, calling my attention to a large red neon sign near the top.

"Recognize that?" he said.

I had seen those interlocking 'C's several times this morning.

"The Charm City logo."

"They used to brew it here. It's where Peter set up shop after Prohibition."

"Looks like it's all lofts now. Why the sign?"

"They call this place Charm City Tower—which is funny, because none of the people living in those lofts would deign to swallow a swig of Charm City. They have taste."

"Can you still get it?" I said.

"Sure, if you want. It's been brewed down in Norfolk for the past twenty-five years. A bigger beer company bought Charm City."

A jingling of bells came from my side of the car. I glanced over as a woman emerged from the door of the florist's shop with a big bouquet of purple mums.

"So this is Wishbone?" I said.

"Oh, no. Wishbone is our next stop."

He turned left in front of Charm City Tower and drove down a street lined with cafés and boutiques. Everyone on the sidewalks seemed to be talking on a cell phone. Which reminded me that I should call Audrey, who expected me home in half an hour. ruthsmom would definitely make the call; she was responsible that way. But Thirsty made the rules of the game I was playing. She reached into the bag and put the phone to sleep.

After two blocks Rusty took another left, pointing us back in the direction of the canal we'd crossed. Before long we recrossed the canal on a bridge that was at least as dubious as the first.

"Now *this* is Wishbone," my guide announced as we rolled off the bridge.

The desolation in Wishbone was different from what we'd traveled through coming in off the freeway. The salvage yards and tow lots in that part of town, grim as they looked, at least had a function. They generated activity, offered a service to the city. Whereas Wishbone seemed utterly and completely spent— a gray ghost town of brick, tin, and steel. Rusty drove me around block after block of industrial buildings, all of them now windowless husks.

We stopped in front of an especially gloomy carapace and Rusty got out. I joined him up near the front bumper of the car.

"Recognize it?" he asked.

"Should I?"

"It was in one of the pictures I showed you back at the library."

"The Justice Lager brewery?"

"That's right. This is where Charm City was brewed before the split. The original recipe, back before Prohibition, when Old Wilhelm was alive." He looked up and down the front of the building. "No way to tell any of that from here."

He set off walking toward the side of the building. It seemed an almost infinite number of awful scenes could unfold here, the vast majority of which began with me deciding to wait alone for Rusty to return. I followed. At the corner of the building a chain-link fence sagged. Rusty walked along the fence, pausing when he'd reached a rent in the wire diamonds. He adroitly stepped through this torn place, then held the fence open as I passed.

"Rusty," I said, gazing across the broken ground between us and the side of the building, "lend me your arm."

He obliged. Slow and steady, my tired legs wobbling on two-inch heels, we worked our way toward the building's outer wall and then followed it toward the rear. At the back corner was a metal door with no knob. Rusty gripped the edge with both hands and heaved. The hinges groaned like a hurt beast.

We entered a vast room full of dust-covered work tables, a few of them standing on their legs, many on their sides or turned upside down, feet in the air. Light streamed in through jagged window holes.

Rusty pulled a pair of small flashlights from his pants' pocket and handed one to me. He pointed toward a metal staircase across the room. "It's not even worth going upstairs. Nothing left up there from the brewing days."

He twisted the end of his flashlight until its yellow bulb ignited. "For our purposes, all the history is down here," he said, leading me to a nearby stairwell. I stood at the top stair and peered down into the mouth of the black shaft. He offered his arm, I took it, and resisted his gentle tug only for an instant before I let him lead me down.

The descent was long; I counted sixty stairs. When we reached the bottom we paused for a moment before setting off across a level cement floor. Our beams carved two tiny tunnels of light.

"How you doing?" he inquired after a time.

"Cold."

"Yeah," he said, pausing, "and there used to be massive

blocks of ice that kept it even colder down here. That's because they were making lager. Back in Germany, lager was conditioned in mountain caves."

"Conditioned?"

"Brewing is about transformation, Thirsty. First you coax all the sugars out of your grain. Then you add your yeast, which turns those sugars into alcohol. Then you put the beer in barrels and bring it down here for conditioning. The cold mellows the flavor."

"Human beings," I marveled.

"People have been brewing beer for thousands of years—since we started growing cereal grains."

Rusty tilted his beam upward and revealed the vaulted structure of the pale ceiling above us. He lowered the beam slightly, pointing out ahead of us, and I saw a row of vaulted arches that receded into the gloom. The beauty of the ceiling surprised me.

"Rusty," I said, "who were these people to you?"

"Karl was my grandfather."

"Did you know him?"

"Only through stories. Peter I knew."

"Peter," I said. "He's the one that brewed swill, but cashed in on the Charm City brand."

"A sweet man, and very rich. But Karl, he wasn't rich. Or sweet."

"I can see why. Did Peter ever offer to help him out?"

"Oh, sure, Peter tried. He knew the taste of Justice Lager wasn't the problem. It was the can."

"The can?" I said.

"Who wants to see a robed, blindfolded woman holding scales and a sword on their *beer* can?"

"I happen to like the way she looks."

"Sure, but you're a historian. A 21st century woman. Not exactly the target audience."

"Point taken," I said.

"Peter told me he had an artist draw up a few new labels he thought might work. Basically, he took the robe off Justice, replaced it with a bikini or something, but kept the blindfold and scales. He had a little fun with it, wanted to push his stodgy brother's buttons. Well, it worked. He showed the sketches to Karl and he was lucky to escape that meeting with his life. It was the last time the two of them ever spoke."

"Have you seen the sketches?"

"I wish. Karl destroyed them. He destroyed everything."

"Everything?"

"Remember I told you about the way Karl guarded the purity of the Rechter yeast?"

"That Old Wilhelm brought from Germany?"

"He basically pulled the plug on Justice Lager after that last meeting with Peter. He disappeared."

"And took the yeast with him?"

"No, he left it behind, totally exposed."

"Why would he do that?"

"Out of spite, I guess. He wanted it corrupted."

A hard shiver shook my body. "Rusty, I need to get out of this place. Now."

He led me back the way we had come. When we reached the bottom of the stairs, a sob escaped me.

"What is it?" Rusty said.

"I shouldn't be here."

"You're not feeling well?"

"It's dark. It's cold. I'm with a stranger, in the middle of a wasteland, underground, at the bottom of sixty steps I can't climb."

"I can help you," he said. "Take my arm again."

"That's not going to be enough."

He stepped up close to me and I threw my arm around his fleshy shoulder. We managed a couple of stairs this way, but barely.

"Maybe we could just"—but before I could finish he had shut his flashlight off and lifted me, one arm beneath my shoulders, the other beneath the crook of my knees, like a groom carrying his bride or a father his sleeping child.

"Is this okay for you?" he asked through clenched teeth.

"Where should I point the light?"

"Just shut it off. I can't see the stairs anyway."

He started working his way up, breathing rhythmically through his nose. The jets of expelled air pressed my linen blouse against the skin of my belly while the smells of Rusty rose to my nostrils. Stale coffee. Deodorant. Grapefruit? I waited for his strength to give out but he kept climbing through the darkness, slow, steady, the rhythm of his steps, the strength of his bulky body lulling me, rocking me, filling my muscles with a sweetness, a lassitude, drawing my eyelids down. I slipped into shallow sleep, believed that Justice Herself held me aloft, a mighty woman, the folds of her gown laying softly over muscles of stone. *Where are we going?* I asked in a child's voice. She looked down at me, eyes uncovered, and her stern features softened, as if she knew me.

The door's groan shook me out of my reverie. I opened my eyes to midday light, the door flapping wide onto the blighted view. The door stayed agape as Rusty set me down and collapsed next to me on the sill, slumped over and panting heavily. I found a tissue in my purse. He took it and began to swab his sweaty forehead.

"Are you all right?" I asked.

He waved the soggy tissue like a flag, too winded to speak.

AFTER A REST, I returned to the car under my own power. Rusty proposed lunch before driving back to Washington. It was nearly two o'clock and I was famished. We drove back across the putrid canal and took a table under the orange awning at Charm City Tower. Rusty ordered a pint of pale ale and a sandwich, and I apologized for not waiting for his food to arrive. I broke out my stash of elk jerky; I had also packed dried cranberries and several fresh plums.

"Rusty," I said, chewing, "you mentioned that people have made beer for as long as they've grown cereal grains."

He nodded. "There are wild yeasts in the air that cause grain to ferment. That only has to happen once for you to know you've got a good thing. Eventually you figure out how to manage the process."

"I can't drink beer," I said.

"I'm sorry."

"See this?" I waved a piece of jerky back and forth. "Wild

deer meat." I lifted up my baggy of cranberries, pointed at my plums. "Hunter-gatherer food's all I consume."

"Is that a political statement?"

"No, it's a health gambit. I've got this…condition." I dug a pen from my bag, wrote two capital letters on a napkin, and lifted it for him to read.

"M?" he said. "S?"

"Run it together."

"Ah, emess."

"That's right. Emphasis on the *mess*."

He frowned. "Your legs?"

"Among other things. It's systemic."

"I shouldn't have taken you down those stairs."

"I didn't have to go."

The server set the pint of pale ale before him—amber body, creamy blond head. It looked delicious.

"Think about this," I said. "Unless you're like my mother-in-law, and you believe people descended from Adam and Eve a few thousand years ago, you know that we're animals, primates that have evolved over millions and millions of years. Consider those millions of years next to the ten thousand or so years since people started farming. What's ten thousand years in the life of the species?"

"A blip."

"So what you have to ask is, how does the body adapt? Before agriculture, we didn't ask the human body to digest cereal grains, we didn't ask it to digest the milk of other animals, let alone the fatty meat of the beasts we raised. Corn-fed beef?" I said. "You've got to be kidding me."

He took a long pull from his glass.

"You know," I said, "there are people who think we invite diseases to attack us because we haven't adapted to the foods we eat."

He lifted a napkin and wiped the foam off his upper lip. "We're off our feed?"

I leaned forward. "You know what? My husband makes fun of the way I eat—calls it the Caveman Diet."

"I do that too," he said.

"Do what?"

"Make fun of things that scare me."

His sandwich arrived and I watched him eat for a moment, his eyes avoiding mine.

"Rusty," I said, "you still haven't asked to see the can."

He set his sandwich on the plate. "I figured you'd show it to me when you were ready."

"Such restraint."

"What's a couple more hours after all these years? A blip."

"You mean you've never seen a Justice Lager can?"

"In the flesh? Oh no. My grandfather took the last ones with him."

I lifted the wrapped can out of my bag and placed it on the table. "Go ahead."

He frowned, wiping his fingers carefully on a napkin. He reached both hands forward and pulled the tissue paper away, layer by layer, until the can lay bare before him. My heart stirred at the sight of Dame Justice. Rusty lifted the can and studied it carefully, rotating it three-hundred-sixty degrees, then checking the top and bottom. His face betrayed no emotion.

I reached over and pointed at the little black bean on Dame Justice's upper arm. "What's your take on this?"

He examined it for a moment, a pale pink coming into his cheeks. "That's a birthmark."

"On Dame Justice?"

"Justice is an abstraction. The woman who modeled for this picture was real. My grandmother Sylvie, who had a dark birthmark on her left arm. Quite a beauty, in her day." He bent over and fished around in his bag a moment, then sat back up and slid an 8 x 10 photograph across the table top. A black-and-white head shot of a serious young woman, full lips, fair hair, a roundness to the jaw that recalled the shape of Rusty's face.

"Karl's wife donned the robe and blindfold?"

"And gripped the scales and sword, yeah." He tipped the glass up and swallowed the rest of his beer. "Remember I told you about the new label Peter suggested?"

"Dame Justice in a bikini?"

"Justice had the birthmark in those drawings too. Karl was convinced Sylvie posed."

"Did she have something going with the artist, or with Peter?"

He shook his head. "No way to know for sure, but I doubt it. Self-pity can breed a lot of things, including paranoia. Karl wasn't the most stable guy."

"Do you know where he disappeared to?"

"Sylvie did. She told me."

"So you knew your grandmother?"

"She raised me, for the most part. Told me a lot of stories.

Once she told me about something she found not long before Karl disappeared. Twenty-four Justice Lager cans on the workbench in their house's basement. They were all capped, but when she picked one up it was much heavier than a can of beer."

"Did she open it?"

"And risk the wrath of Karl? No. But she noticed that when Karl disappeared, those cans went with him."

I slapped the table with both hands.

"Everything all right?" Rusty asked.

"You said they found something when they started dredging for the Fort McHenry Tunnel. Part of a body."

He closed his eyes. "A leg, to be precise. The remains of one."

"And let me guess. It had cans attached to it."

"Cone top cans," he said, nodding. "Twelve of them, full of sand."

"Justice Lager cans?"

"No way to tell after decades in salt water. But Sylvie knew."

"Did she try to verify whose leg it was?"

"Nope."

"Why not?"

"I asked her that. She said she was an old woman by then, worn out from raising three children by herself. As far as she was concerned, Karl could stay disappeared."

"She raised you also, didn't you say?"

"She lived in my parents' house. They left us alone most of the time."

We were quiet as the server cleared.

"Rusty," I said, "how long have you been collecting cans?"

"Twenty years, give or take."

"When you go out dumping, is it a Justice Lager can you're searching for?"

He looked at his lap. "Justice Lager took a lot away from her. Maybe that's why my grandmother liked the idea of me finding one of those cans. She died before I could get it done. What was I going to do, stop searching?"

"You can stop now."

He showed me his palms. "I dump cans, I trade cans, but I can't afford to buy them."

"Who said anything about buying?"

"You've got a valuable can there. We've both seen what those knuckleheads are bidding for it. Sell it to one of them."

"Consider it a trade."

"What would I give you?"

I laughed. "I'd still be underground if you hadn't carried me out. You could have left me down there in the dark."

Before he could answer I silenced him with an enormous yawn. Fatigue always hit me hard after the midday meal. When the yawn concluded I told him to hurry and finish his sandwich. It was time for my game to end.

IN THE CAR, I told Rusty I wanted to go back to Washington, the Capitol South Metro station. But then I changed my mind. "I'm really worn out," I said. "Do you think you could drive me home?"

He said it wouldn't be a problem. I told him to set a course for Cleave Springs and propped my head against the window. I was out before we'd crossed the canal—and back in the arms of Dame Justice again, the meal I'd just shared with Rusty only a break in the middle of a dream that had begun on the brewery's basement stairs. Once again I felt Her strong arms under me. I looked up into that chiseled face, the quiet lips, the regal nose, the eyes that had softened for me earlier. *Do you know me?* my child voice asked. She looked down, reacting to the sound, and I understood instantly that the eyes were useless—blank ovals of buffed stone. *Can you see me?* I said anyway. *I thought you saw me.* The next thing I knew Rusty was shaking my shoulder.

"Sorry," he said. "I tried to be gentle, but you were pretty zonked."

I sat up and looked around, blinking away the dream. We were on the Avenue, not far from my house. I directed him around the last corner and had him pull to the curb a couple of houses before mine.

"Well," he said, "we've had quite a day."

"Haven't we. I'm tempted to invite you in and introduce you to the family."

For the first time all day, he laughed—a strange, whinnying sound. "Your family hasn't seen you since morning."

"You're probably right." I took hold of the door handle, but the discomfort I'd heard in his laugh gave me pause. I let my fingers fall into my lap. "One thing, though. I couldn't tell what you were feeling when you first laid eyes on the Justice Lager can. You looked like a can collector appraising a can. I was just wondering if finally having this one made you feel anything."

He turned his face away.

"Two things, actually," I said. "Is Rusty your real name?"

"I should have known," he said to the window.

"Known what?"

"You sure you want to do this?"

"Do what?"

"Is Thirsty *your* name?"

I laughed. "Isn't that obvious?"

"We had a deal," he said sharply, turning his face to the windshield. "Are you backing out?"

"You have the can."

"And you have your story."

"Story?"

"What do you want now?" he said. "The truth?"

"You mean?"

He exhaled loudly, letting his head fall back against the rest.

"You played me," I said, and watched as his face darkened toward deepest purple. A big tear welled from the eye nearest me and rolled swiftly down his cheek.

"Mid-Atlantic cone tops are the focus of my whole collection. A mint condition Justice Lager cone top is the holy grail for a guy like me. When I saw what people were bidding for it, people who have no real knowledge, no true appreciation for that can, I just couldn't stand it. I knew I'd never be able to buy one. And then you sent me that email asking for information about Justice Lager. I figured you might be the person who put that can up for auction. And when I found out you *were* that person, I thought I might have a chance to meet up with you, see the can people like me dream about. Maybe work out a trade."

"I told you up front I don't collect beer cans."

"Did that mean I had nothing to offer? Value has many forms."

We were quiet a moment. "So," I said, "you made up everything?"

He shook his head. "Most of the history is real. I researched Justice Lager a couple of years ago and wrote it up in case I ever had the chance to feature it as Can of the Month. I reviewed it all before we met. And then I saw what you were after. You were going to need to know everything. But some things just aren't known. They can't be known. So I started making them up."

"Which things?"

"Karl's disappearance is one of the big blank spots in the history. I've never been able to learn what happened to him, or to the Rechter yeast. But you gave me a great idea when you started talking about the Fort McHenry Tunnel. What if Karl drowned himself, took the last Justice Lager cans down with him?"

"What about Sylvie?"

"That *was* the name of Karl's wife."

"And the picture you showed me at lunch?"

He frowned. "My grandmother. I was looking for a way to work her in, and when you asked about that mark you just handed it to me on a platter."

"You wanted to work your grandmother in?"

"I figured you might trade with me if I made it personal enough."

"So there was no birthmark on Sylvie's arm?"

"Not to my knowledge."

"God damn. I believed you."

"Because you wanted to. You were dying to make me whole."
He turned toward me and reached between the front seats, back
to the rear of the car. After a moment he pivoted back around
and dropped the wrapped can in my lap.

I STOOD ON THE SIDEWALK looking across the yard and in
through the front windows of my house. The house next door
blocked the late day sun, so Audrey had turned on the light above
the dining room table, where she was standing next to Ruth looking down at the food on the plate of dinner she had just served.
Ruth was upset, pointing an emphatic finger at the plate; Audrey's
shoulders slumped with fatigue. In the front room, Zach sat on
the couch reading his magazine, taut as a twist of wire, doing his
best to ignore the squabble in the next room and keep the lid on
his worries about what might have happened to me.

With this tableau before me, I walked through what would
happen if I entered the front door right now. First my abject
apologies to Zach and Audrey, their angry relief. Then an abun-
dance of guilty affection showered on Ruth, who would treat me
roughly for the rest of the evening and forget the whole thing
by tomorrow. Within thirty minutes of my return this weird day
would begin to right itself like a boat after a squall, my absence
only briefly blowing the family off its customary course.

I walked over to the driveway that runs along the side of the
house, heading back to the detached garage where Zach works
on the bikes. I entered the little building and shut the door tightly
behind me. The space was tidy, organized, with tires and wheels

dangling from overhead hooks and various families of tools arrayed on the pegboard walls. Bikes at different stages of assembly crowded the corners. I went to a clear space on the workbench and removed the Justice Lager can from my purse.

I laid the can on its side and searched the walls for the proper tool. At length I closed the fingers of my right hand around the wooden handle of a hammer, its blunt metal nose balanced by a forked claw. I raised the hammer above my head and brought it down with all the force I could muster, grunting loudly, leaving a deep dent at Justice's hip. My right arm felt surprisingly strong. I swung again, again, again, each time vocalizing on impact, my noises changing as the pummeling continued, growls of vengeful pleasure giving way in the end to wails.

I kept at it until she was flat as a piece of road kill.

The hammer back on its peg, the carcass in my bag, I closed the garage door and followed the driveway back up to the front of the house. Inside the front door I stood and listened for a moment, Ruth's chatty tone telling me that Audrey had calmed her. Zach looked up from his magazine and I put my finger to my lips, tipping my head toward the stairs.

I was on our bed when Zach closed the bedroom door behind him. He stayed on that side of the room.

I waved him over. "Help me, will you?"

He came and pulled the pumps off my feet, helped me hoist my legs up onto the bed. I lay on my side, head and shoulders propped on pillows.

"You're exhausted," he said.

"I am."

"You should have been here hours ago. We had no idea what happened. Ruth kept asking for you. Mom called in sick to her other job. She was beside herself."

"I should have called," I said, closing my eyes.

"Why the hell didn't you?"

I exhaled slowly, then opened my eyes. "I wanted to disappear."

He unfolded his arms and raised them above his shoulders briefly before dropping his hands to his hips. "Oh, okay. You wanted to disappear."

"You do it every day, Zachary."

"That's not true. You know where I've gone, when I'm coming back."

"But while you're running, you're gone. You're inside something, and it's not this."

He shifted his weight from one leg to the other. His eyes stayed on me.

"Meanwhile, I'm here. Disappearing."

"Don't talk like that," he said. "You have a long time ahead of you."

"Too much, if this is how it's going to be."

I asked him to hand me the bottle of water that stood on the night-stand.

"It's very rare," I said after a long drink.

"What is?"

"The Justice Lager can."

"Do I care about that can right now?"

"You never cared about it, but I did. So I found out about it."

He waited.

"Three mortgage payments," I said. "As of this morning, that's the top bid. Three more months."

"Damn. That's a lot of money for a beer can."

"We're not going to sell it," I said.

"Like hell we're not. We need that money."

"Hand me my bag, will you."

He lifted the bag from the floor and set it on the bed next to me. I pulled out the flattened can to show him.

"Holy fuck!" he shouted. "What happened to it?"

"I happened to it."

He pointed. "You did that?"

"Me. The woman who used to support you by doing the work she loved. Who stopped doing that work when she had your child. Who couldn't go back to it because she began to disintegrate. The woman whose food you mock, whose body you're scared to hold. The mother who can barely pick up her own child, who hates her helpful mother-in-law because she *can* pick up the child, twirl her. Actually, she hates all of you—Zachary, Audrey, Ruth. She hates you for being well when she's not. She wishes you were sick and she was well and could take care of you. That's how it should be. That's how it would be if there were such a thing as justice."

He sat down heavily on the edge of the bed, looking the way I'd felt in the car a little while before, after Rusty had revealed how desperate I'd become for something to believe.

But I don't get it, I'd said to Rusty before he drove off. *If you wanted to steal the can from me, why didn't you just take my bag and leave me down in that basement?*

Carrying you up those stairs was part of our deal, he said.

I get a day in Baltimore, a tangled yarn, and you get a valuable collector's item. What kind of deal is that?

I wouldn't have taken the can if I'd thought it was unfair. My mistake was trying to trade with someone in your condition.

My condition?

Sorry, he said. *I can't make you whole, either.*

"Zachary?" I said after a while.

"What is it?"

"Did you know that there's wild yeast in the air, floating all around us, right now? It's too tiny to see, but it's there."

"Is it?"

"And do you know what that means?" I said, yawning.

"What?"

"Things will change."

I closed my eyes and rolled onto my back. This was the place, the porous frontier of sleep, where I sometimes remembered what it was like to be blind. That first time Ruth was still a small baby, five or six months old. Each evening I would stand at the kitchen sink with Zach nearby to make sure she was safe. The soap brought a soothing mix of herbs to my nose, aloe and calendula, lavender and chamomile. I would lather her carefully, my fingers sliding into the little folds of fat under her chin and around her upper thighs, across her tight belly, up along the delicate ridge of her spine. I would rinse her with cups of warm water, cooing back to her. After the bath, I would wrap her in a thick cotton towel to dry off before laying her out on the towel so my fingertips could wander through the silk on her head, down to trace the outlines of eyes and nose, cheeks and mouth and chin. The oil's fragrance was softer than the soap's, muted and musky. I would begin working it into the skin of her belly and move outward from there, along each limb, pausing at each joint on the way out to anoint every tiny finger and toe.

But now mine was the body being touched. Hands began rubbing my tired feet through the sheer fabric of my knee-high hose. My hose slipped away, the left one first, next the right, and the hands touched my bare feet, kneading. I was tempted to open my eyes, to make sure I wasn't dreaming, but chose to trust what I was feeling as the hands reached up and under me, tugging on the elastic waist of my pants, sliding them down and away. They traveled up my bare legs, not kneading anymore, but lightly grazing. Fingertips trailed over the skin, tracing characters on my ankles, calves, knees, moving upward over my thighs, rising, flowing up toward the core of me like bubbles rising inside a glass.

The Hank Williams Dialogues

"BLUE BIRDY, DADDY! I want blue birdy!"

"Hang on," I say to Max as I fiddle with the straps of his car seat, "blue birdy's on the way."

I get myself buckled in and switch on the stereo. Slow slide guitar takes us out of the driveway, and then Hank's sorrowful voice comes in:

> *Hear that lonesome whippoorwill*
> *He sounds too blue to fly*
> *The midnight train is whining low*
> *I'm so lonesome I could cry*

"Is this a sad song?" the boy asks.

"It is a sad song."

"No it's not," he says. "It's a *lonely* song."

"Well, sometimes being lonely can make you sad." I brake gently, creeping past a stop sign.

"Why is the birdy lonely?"

"I don't know," I say, "but maybe your brother does. After all, he is in first grade."

We both wait hopefully for Nicholas to speak, but he is mum.

"He's lonely because he misses his birdy friends," Max says. "Maybe that's why."

"He *does* miss them," he insists, threatening tears.

"Yes he does." I round the first corner and speed up, swinging left to pass a car that's stopped at the curb, hazards blinking.

"Daddy?"

"Yes, love?"

"Is Hank going to cheer the birdy up?"

I tell him that's exactly what Hank's going to do. Right. At 29, Hank died alone in the back seat of a limousine with a few cans of beer and a handwritten song.

"He's a blue birdy," Max observes.

"But not the color blue," I say, braking. At the stoplight, I swivel in my seat and look back at my boys. Nicholas sits behind the passenger seat, the booster beneath his butt lifting him high enough to use the car's shoulder strap. He stares grimly out his window. Max, on the driver's side, is getting too big for his toddler seat. "Get this," I say to him. "Blue also means sad."

Hank may be launching into the fourth and final verse, wrapping up this song, but we're still glossing the first two lines. While Max chews on my last assertion I close my eyes a moment, scanning the family bookshelf for a supporting example. "Think of Curious George."

"Curious George is brown," he points out, and the light changes. We're moving again.

"True, but remember the time he was riding his bike along the stream, looking at all the boats he'd made out of newspapers, not watching where he was going, and he hit that rock?"

"It wasn't a stream. It was a river."

"And his bike was broken. And he couldn't ride, and he couldn't carry it, and what did he do?"

"He cried," the boy says in a small voice.

"He was feeling blue." I pull up to the curb in front of Cleave Springs Elementary. "Just like the lonesome whippoorwill. Now say goodbye to your brother."

I grab Nicholas' backpack from the seat next to mine and go around the car to meet him. I remind him that his mother will pick him up. Kneeling down, I take his shoulders in my hands, fishing for some eye contact but not even getting a nibble.

Have a great day, I might say to him if the possibility didn't seem so remote. Instead I tell him to have a decent one.

I DRIVE MAX OVER to the preschool and walk him inside. Chiming welcomes me back to the car.

"Jambalaya," I say into the flipped-open phone, and give Harriet a few beats to respond. "You don't like it."

"I like jambalaya," she says. "It's delicious, when it's cooked right. But as a name? For a restaurant owned by us?"

"That's the idea we've been toying with."

"*We've?*"

On Depot, our first Cleave Springs restaurant, Harriet took the lead because it was her idea and I was still working on Capitol Hill. On Black Iris, over in Beverly, we worked as equal partners even though Nicholas was nursing. But since Max was born she's focused on the home front while I've taken on more and more of the responsibilities for our growing empire. Still, I'm not ready to face this third one alone.

"I got the name from the Hank Williams song," I say, her silence telling me this information soothes her. "Most of Hank's tunes are dreary, but "Jambalaya" is about good times."

"You listen to Hank Williams?"

"Not closely, before now. I was thinking about restaurant names the other day and "Jambalaya" popped into my head. I bought a CD so I could see if it sounded the way I remembered it. Have you noticed that Max is getting hooked on Hank?"

"He keeps talking about some blue bird."

"The lonesome whippoorwill," I say, pulling out of the lot. "What's up with Nicholas? He won't talk."

"He's brooding about something."

"I brooded too, but when my parents spoke to me I answered."

"*We've*," Harriet says again, and I just wait. "What makes you think she knows anything about designing a new restaurant?"

"She studied design in college. This is professional experience for her and a bargain for us."

"You know who she worked for, don't you?"

"I know she worked for Big Boss Man."

"You know what she did, right?"

"Should I ask him? We're meeting first thing."

"He's a rat," Harriet says. "You can tell him I said so."

"Consider it done."

She tells me that Max has a doctor's appointment at 1:30 today, his three-year-old visit, which means I'm picking Nicholas up from school. "I hope you remembered that."

"Me, forget?"

"That's a laugh," she says, not laughing. "Listen, are you going back out after stories again tonight?"

"Have to. I'm interviewing another chef."

She sighs. "We need to talk."

Harriet doesn't work inside restaurants these days, but she watches the balance sheets like Dutchmen watch dykes. It's too early in the day for me to hear about a leak.

"Aren't we talking right now?"

"No," she says, "we're not."

BIG BOSS MAN rules Cleave Springs from the white, four-door pickup truck that's waiting for me when I pull into the parking lot behind the building. I take a spot near his and watch him climb down from the high cab.

"Hank Williams," he says, having heard the music through my open windows. "Your cheating heart will tell on you."

"So I've heard."

He watches me closely from under the bill of his cap, like he's looking at me—really looking—for the first time. "Hank Williams?"

I nod toward the manila folder in his hand. "You have that lease?"

"Let's go inside."

I follow him around to the front of the building and he opens the boarded-up front door. It's the old bank building, the plum property on the Avenue, and the only space on Cleave Springs' main drag that hasn't already been cleaned up and leased to a business that caters to the people who can afford what houses in our neighborhood cost these days. Two years ago I tracked down and tried to do a deal with the owner of this elegant, crumbling edifice, a crazy old woman hooked up to an oxygen tank. She sent me packing without ever naming her price. A few months ago, when I heard she'd sold to Big Boss Man, I instantly saw him standing in the sick room in his heavy brown boots, looming above the old woman's wasted body, one of his burly hands clutching the fragile oxygen tube like he might start to whip her with it, the other hand offering her the pen she would use to sign the property over to him.

The guy knows how much the space thrills me because I made the mistake of telling him so the first time we came in here together. Even with the tall, arched windows boarded over, even with the mold stains on the walls, even with the only light coming from two naked bulbs that dangle from the high ceiling, I come in here and all I can see is what a happening place Jambalaya will be.

"Another restaurant," he says.

"Restaurant and bar."

"You don't think the Avenue's already saturated?"

"My whole plan is predicated on Cleave Springs becoming a destination."

"Predicated," he says.

"Depot, the other places on the Avenue, they're mostly serving the people who live here. But people from everywhere will want to come to this new joint."

"They'll want to come because...?"

"There's a sweet spot between funky and fine. I know how

to find it. Now," I say, reaching toward the folder, "are you going to let me see that lease?"

His phone chimes as he's handing me the folder. He starts talking and heads for the door, motioning for me to come with him. He locks the door behind us and I walk back toward the parking lot with him, scanning the lease as I go. When we reach his pickup, he flips the phone shut and tells me he's got to run.

"One minute. These numbers are all wrong."

He climbs up onto the seat of the truck and shuts the door. "Call me," his lips say as the engine roars to life.

"PREDICATED," I SAY. "What's wrong with the word 'predicated'?"

"He's threatened by you," Crystal says. She sits next to me in the booth in Depot's front dining room that I've occupied all morning. Her fabric swatches, six-inch squares, make a neat stack on the table and her thigh presses lightly against mine. The lunch servers whisk around the room, getting things ready for the noon rush.

"Threatened?"

"All that fancy education." She lifts the swatch at the top of her stack, which is way too orange.

I shake my head. "Did you threaten him too? I could see him having trouble dealing with a smart young woman."

"Secretary is a support position. I played that role, and we got along fine." These last words are pitch-perfect, no trace in them of the stories that swirl about Crystal leaving her job under pressure from Big Boss Man's wife.

"And you left because…?"

"Because I don't want to be a secretary when I grow up."

"What *do* you want to be?"

She holds up another swatch. "This is nice."

"This color," I say, "or this job?"

"Both. I like working for you and Harriet, but I don't want to serve forever."

"This was our first restaurant," I say, lifting the salt and pepper caddy off the table, a little steam engine made of homey hammered tin.

Crystal toots like a locomotive. Her mouth is playful, her pale brown eyes as hard as walnut shells.

I set the caddy down. "Harriet wanted the train motif because Cleave Springs started out as a rail workers' neighborhood."

"All aboard," Crystal says.

"My leverage was limited back then. Hadn't quit the day job yet. But I did manage to put the brakes on a couple of bad ideas."

"Like?"

"Engineer hats for the servers. Every booth a little boxcar."

She grimaces as if from shooting pains.

"Jambalaya will be different," I say. "We'll do it right. You'll get a lot of experience, set yourself up for another design job. I know you pulled the dinner shift last night. Thanks for coming in this morning."

"Thank you," she says, and it's the weight she puts on *you*, the suggestion that I've already given her more than I know, that sends me back to the lease on the table in front of me. For the

third time since we parted earlier, I call Big Boss Man. Straight
to voicemail again.

"Could it be a test?" she says after I slap the phone shut.

"How bad do I want it, you mean?"

She nods. "Do you want it more than the other guy?"

"The other guy? Do you know something?"

"Only how he operates."

"So you think someone else wants to lease the space?"

"Or use it," she says, tilting her head.

"What, he wants to open a business himself?"

"He's got time on his hands. It's not like Cleave Springs has
many properties left to flip."

"True," I say, remembering how he quizzed me about my
business plan this morning. "Crystal, is he thinking about opening a restaurant?"

She raises another swatch, this one the color of kidney beans.

"Do I know what he's thinking?"

I nod, but not because the color is right.

LUNCH AT DEPOT IS BUSY. The crowd's convivial roar travels up
the stairwell and through the open door of my office, where I
sit reading chefs' resumes. The phone barely has a chance to
chime before I flip it open. "He's fucking with the numbers."

"Surprise, surprise," Harriet says. "Competition?"

"Of one kind or another. Where are you?"

"Just picked up Max. He's distraught because Hank is in your
car. Can you talk to him?" The phone tumbles from hand to
hand.

"Daddy?" The boy's voice teeters on the edge of grief.

"Hi, sweetheart. How was school?"

"Daddy?"

"Here I am."

"I want Goodbye Joe, Daddy."

I was never a good singer, but fatherhood has made me a willing one. "You want Goodbye Joe? Get ready, big boy. Here it comes."

> *Goodbye Joe, me got to go, me oh my oh*
> *Me got to go pole the pirogue down the bayou*
> *My Yvonne the sweetest one me oh my oh*
> *Son of a gun we'll have good fun on the bayou*

When I sing most artists' songs, I'm acutely, even painfully aware of my voice's complete lack of range and color. Hank's songs are different. Something inside them numbs my critical ear. I'm the one singing this tune, but it's Hank's cracked timbre that I hear, as if the jaunty phrases he unfurls, the fresh emotions that set them alight, have welled up this very moment from my own soul.

Knowing my listener as I do, I stop at the end of the first verse for a bit of exegesis. As usual, he wants to know if a pirogue is a boat, and I confirm that it is. He wants to know if the bayou is water, he wants to know if Yvonne is Hank's friend, he wants to know if there's going to be a party on the bayou and if Hank and Yvonne are going to the party and if there's going to be cake. I answer every question in the affirmative.

"Daddy?" he says.

"Yes, love."

"Where are you, Daddy?"

"At Depot, working. I'll see you for stories."

"I'm going to choose a book," he says.

"Only one?"

"Two books!"

"And I'm going to read them to you."

The phone tumbles from hand to hand again. "Remember," Harriet says. "You're picking up Nicholas."

I'M REHEARSING MONOLOGUES as I lean against my idling car. When the herd of first-graders bursts through the double doors and comes rumbling across the playground, I don't even try to catch sight of mine. I know he's behind the pack, going at his own pace, this boy who reads circles around his peers but could use a tutor's help to master the basics of walking. Harriet is probably right to see his gangly, tentative gait as a purely physical problem, his body slower than most at coordinating itself. I take his steps more personally, seeing too much of myself in the walk of a boy who can't quite trust the earth to support him.

Most of the other cars have launched by the time he arrives, his crabbed, halting steps out of sync with the look of fierce concentration that grips his face. "Hello, handsome," I say, relieving him of his pack. "I was wrong when I told you Mommy would pick you up. She had to take your brother to the doctor for his check up."

I toss the pack on the passenger's seat, sit down behind the wheel, and wait until I hear his seatbelt click shut. "Everything

all right?" I say, pulling away from the curb. "How was school?"
I check the rearview and see him staring out his window.

What, I could say, *you want to scare me off so you can get into the restaurant business yourself? It's a tough business, very tough. What do you know about creating a scene people will like? What do you know about developing a concept, hiring a chef, naming cocktails? It's nothing like being a contractor, believe me. If you do this, you'll fail.*

Okay, I could say, *you want a piece of the action? That's reasonable. You've got the space, I've got the concept, the experience. Tell you what*, I could say, *you put up half the capital, I'll put up the other half. Let's be partners.*

But you don't want to collaborate with me, do you? You want to give me a choice: walk away or fail. Either way, you're still the king. Well, I could say, *good try, asshole. I'm not intimidated. I'm not backing down. Get ready to lose your throne.*

When I pull up in front of the house Harriet's wagon is there, back already from the doctor's. I check Nicholas' face in the rearview, and something about the squint of his eyes tells me to hold my tongue, to sit tight and give him a minute before I take him to the front door.

"I was wondering," he says.

"Yes?" I wait several beats, willing myself to stay quiet, be patient, but he's gone silent as a stone. "What were you wondering, love?"

He releases the seatbelt and opens his door. I grab his backpack and step around to meet him, going with him up the walkway and onto the front porch. "Are you going to tell me?" I say, and the squint of his eyes says he's still thinking about it.

But Harriet opens the front door, and the moment dissolves.

CRYSTAL, IN WHITE BLOUSE and black slacks, dressed to serve, pops into my office before starting the dinner shift. She drops a furniture catalogue on my desktop and rests her hands there, bending at the waist, her pale brown eyes level with mine. "Some nice pieces for the bar in there. I marked a bunch of pages."

"Thanks, I'll look at them."

"We really have to get back in there with a tape measure. I need to be in the space to know if some of these pieces will work."

"If Big Boss Man wasn't AWOL, we could try to get the key."

"Ah, the key." She reaches into the pocket of her slacks and pulls out a gold key on a white string.

"How'd you get that?"

"He's not entirely AWOL."

"Just from me?"

She reaches back and slides the key into her pocket. "The more time you have to wonder, the less certain you get."

"Here's what I'm getting uncertain about," I say. "You."

"Me?"

"Crystal, who are you working for?"

She lifts her hands from the desktop and stands upright. "You sign my checks."

"The key," I say. "Why'd he give it to you?"

She shrugs. "I asked, he gave."

"No strings?"

"Hard to imagine," she says, nodding.

"Impossible, actually. But here's what I *can* imagine. You know one of us is going to open a restaurant in that building. You don't care who it is. Either way, you're going to be involved."

"Half right," she says.

"Okay, what am I wrong about?"

She plants her hands on the desk top again, this time leaning in close enough that I can smell her shampoo. "I do care."

We hold each other's gaze a moment before she backs away, standing upright again. "Will you be here when I finish? I thought we could go over there tonight."

"I'm interviewing that chef from Serpentine. I'll hang out till you're done."

HARRIET HAS JUST FINISHED getting the freshly bathed boys into their pajamas when I arrive. It's her turn to read to Nicholas tonight, so I cozy up with Max on his bed, a head of fragrant brown curls propped on my chest. The child knows every word of the six or eight books that currently hold his interest, and I make sport with his memory while I read, occasionally veering away from the text so he can catch and correct me.

Two books, a little chit-chat, and the separation dance begins. I move his head from my chest to the pillow. I pull the white blanket up over him first, then the green blanket. Froggy goes on the pillow next to him, otter goes between him and the wall, but walrus sleeps on the floor. I move to the chair near the bed.

"How about the window song? Haven't sung you that one in a while."

"Window song!"

"Let's see if I remember the words." I close my eyes a moment, waiting for the intro to materialize in my head. I hear the plaintive guitar, and then my being starts to fill with Hank's forlorn sound:

> *You're window shoppin*
> *Just window shoppin*
> *You're only lookin around*
> *You're not buyin*
> *You're just tryin*
> *To find the best deal in town*

"Who is Hank talking to?" Max wants to know.

"To a friend, I think."

"Is his friend a girl or a boy?"

"I'm guessing his friend is a woman."

"She's going to buy a window?"

"Not exactly. Window shopping means shopping for something when you don't plan to buy just yet. It's an expression."

He chews on that for a moment. "What is Hank's friend shopping for?"

"She's shopping for a man," I say. "But it's kind of tricky. People can't be bought like things in a store, so if this woman is looking for a good deal, it's not exactly the lowest price she wants." I stand up. "I'm not making much sense, am I?"

"Daddy?" Max says, yawning.

"Yes, love."

"Is Hank angry?"

"It sounds to me like he's more sad than angry."

"It's a blue song?"

"It *is* a blue song." I bend down to kiss his forehead. "Now it's time for Daddy to say goodnight."

"I want Mommy to say goodnight, too."

I go to the doorway of Nicholas' room, where a familiar tableau awaits me: dim lamplight, books strewn about bed and floor, son cleaving to mother, both asleep. I tiptoe across the floor and touch Harriet's arm. Usually she awakens instantly, but today, like yesterday and the day before, she doesn't even move. I shake her lightly, then harder. The eyes open, slowly the brain engages. She yawns, blinks several times, and slithers out of the boy's grasp.

"He wants the bank building for himself," I whisper to her in the hall.

"For what?"

"Wants to open his own restaurant."

"Let him," she laughs.

"But that's competition for Depot."

"I doubt it. The guy's a contractor—a bad one, I might add." She glances down the hall toward our bathroom, where we spent two thousand bucks on plumbing a month after Big Boss Man sold us our "fully renovated" house. "What makes you think he can run a good restaurant?"

"Mommy?" Max calls. "I want Mommy to say goodnight."

Harriet tells him she'll be right there.

"We need to *talk* about this," I say, clinching annoyance in both fists.

"We *do* need to talk," she says gravely. "Wake me up when you come in."

❖ ❖ ❖

THE CHEF SPORTS A MANE of wavy black hair and a small silver hoop in each ear. The stubble on his face is a few days from becoming a beard. Facing me across one of Depot's bar tables, he leans in to listen as I weave my Jambalaya vision. It's not a Cajun restaurant that I've got in mind, not some greasy spoon in the French Quarter where you go for gumbo and red beans and rice. No, it's an *inflection* I'm after, a Jambalaya spirit of good times, good people, and creative, authentic, down-to-earth food.

The chef sees what I'm saying, or claims to. Halfway through the second martini he begins to speak, discoursing on the versatility of oysters and shrimp, the mysterious properties of andouille sausage, the untapped possibilities of okra. Somewhere in the middle of this Crystal appears, her hair down, the white shirt less buttoned than before. The dinner shift must be over.

She joins us for a drink. I start to tell the chef about the bank space, but before I get very far I remember that Crystal has the key.

We quickly empty our glasses. I grab my briefcase and off we go down the Avenue, where the cool night air on my face and the solid sidewalk beneath my happy feet make me understand for the first time how buzzed I am. I buzz to my companions about Cleave Springs, this blighted little neighborhood that we've brought back to life. The big stucco house on our right is a salon and spa called Revive. Thugs used to congregate on the porch of this falling-down place, the thumping woofers in their cars rattling the teeth of all who passed. The Lily Pad Café occupies the ground floor of the neighborhood's original department store. After the department store closed a series of churches passed through the building. When the last congregation left, it became the crack house it was when Big Boss Man sold Harriet and me our house. These days the Lily Pad bustles every morning with well-dressed babies and moms who hold advanced degrees.

"And now for the next big thing," I say as we arrive at the boarded up bank building. Crystal unlocks the door and turns on the lights. We give the chef a tour of the space, talking him through the layout—bar up front, dining room in the center, kitchen tucked under the loft we plan to build in the back. He loves our idea of turning the old bank vault into a wine cellar. As Crystal starts to take some measurements I walk the chef out to the street, querying him on the brands of equipment he favors, showing him the kind of owner I'll be, how I'll listen, support, facilitate.

Back inside, I don't see Crystal. I walk around the space a minute before I notice a light coming from the doorway of the vault in the back corner. I find her in the fortified room, sitting on a little ledge that runs along one wall, the catalogue open on her lap.

"I needed better light," she says.

I go to sit down beside her, but misjudge the height of the ledge and lunge sidelong against her. "Sorry," I say, but don't scoot away.

She closes the catalogue. "Well?"

"I think he's the guy. His references are stellar, he's ready to run his first kitchen, and he digs our concept. I like him. What do you think?"

"I missed most of the interview," she says in a voice that might be cross.

"Oh," I say, "you want to interview chefs with me, too?"

Her face swivels away from me.

I lean in, closing the little gap she's opened between us. "That came out wrong. I just don't want to presume anything, Crystal. What I meant to ask is how much do you want to be involved in?"

"Everything," she says, turning to me again, her eager voice reaching in to shake a part of me that used to come awake whenever I was with Harriet, a part of me made vibrant by the light of my wife's attention.

Everything. Is that what I have, or is it what I want? It's what I'm ready to give to be everything to someone again.

"Crystal," I say, lifting her hand to my mouth.

She yanks her hand away and stands, glaring down at me.

"What are you doing?"

I have no answer.

Her neck is scarlet, her eyes murky with affront. "Did you think?"

"But you said…"

"What did I say?"

"That you *did* care who opened a restaurant here. I thought you were saying you wanted it to be me."

"Not because I want you to kiss my *hand*." She walks to the door of the vault, peering out to the main room.

"Crystal, I'm so sorry."

She stays in the doorway, looking out.

"I thought you were interested in me. I wanted you to be."

"I *was* interested in you," she says, facing me again. "I *am* interested in you. I'm interested in *working* with you."

The disappointment on her face sends my eyes to my feet. I'm still looking down when she says, "Can I ask you something?"

"Anything."

"Would you ever, in a million years, open a restaurant with plaid table cloths?"

"He likes plaid?" I say, looking up at her again.

She nods gloomily. "His roots are in Scotland."

"I see it now. Hairy-legged waiters running around in kilts. All you can eat haggis. Intimate candle light dinners with live bagpipe music."

We laugh a little. She comes back and sits down, leaving a good foot of space between us.

"Not that it's any of my business," I say.

She shakes her head. "No, never. He worries about me, like a daughter or something. People see the way he acts around me and jump to conclusions."

I tip my head toward the rhythmic sound of boot steps thudding across the main room. "He protects you?"

"From wolves," Crystal says as Big Boss Man fills the doorway of the vault.

"I was driving by," he says. "Saw the front door ajar."

I stand up. "You're out late."

"You too," he says. "Hi Cryssie."

Crystal raises her catalogue. "We were talking about furniture, taking some measurements."

"Restaurant furniture," he says. "Can I see?"

Crystal hands him the catalogue and he starts thumbing through it.

"Is your phone broken?" I ask him. "I've been calling you all day about the lease."

"Is there a problem?"

"Only that the numbers on there aren't the ones we agreed on."

"They're not," he says, his tone falling somewhere between statement and question.

I open my briefcase. "Take a look," I say, handing over the document before I sit back down on the ledge.

He quickly scans the pages. "Those are the numbers."

"Pretty high, don't you think?"

"I've got numbers to make too," he says. "This building wasn't gifted to me."

"Of course not."

He pinches the bill of his cap and adjusts it, making his eyes more visible. "Listen, if this little thing of yours can't crank those kind of numbers, fine. I'll work out something else." He rolls the lease up into a loose cylinder. "That way, the two of you can go home and get to sleep, which is what I'm about to do." He turns to go, but pauses. "Cryssie, you need a ride home?"

"Oh," she says, "thanks."

I stand. "Wait a minute. We're not done here."

Neither of them moves as I pull from my shirt pocket the gold pen my mother gave me when I finished law school. "I've got some papers to sign." I take the rolled-up lease from Big Boss Man and sit down on the ledge, briefcase across my knees, heart pounding ferociously as I flip through the pages and scrawl my signature boldly above my printed name.

"I guess that's done," Crystal says, pleased.

Big Boss Man smiles. "Not quite."

"Harriet has to sign it too," I explain, and Crystal's darkening face tells me I've surprised her a second time.

The three of us walk out together, Crystal locking the door and then handing the key to Big Boss Man. The white pickup sits curbside. After they climb into it, I approach Big Boss Man's door and his window slides down. "You're a Hank Williams fan," I say, intent that he, too, should be surprised just once before this day is done. "I'll bet you know this one."

Before he can respond, I start singing the words I've already sung once tonight, and they rise up out of me as raw and woeful as when I sang them in Max's bedroom.

"Don't worry," I say when I finish, stepping up on the truck's running board, "you'll know tomorrow."

"Know what?" they both ask.

"Who's got the best deal in town."

I'M TOO KEYED UP to read or watch TV or even to comb the Web for further details of Hank's biography. I'm about to open the liquor cabinet when I remember that Harriet wanted me to wake her.

Upstairs, I switch on the bedside lamp and find Nicholas sleeping in my place. I lift his limp body and carry him back to his own bed. Harriet is in the grip of the same aggressive sleep I interrupted earlier this evening. It takes me a full minute to rouse her, and when I finally do she regards me with a look that begins in alarm and ends in accusation.

"What happened?" she says.

"You said to wake you when I got in."

She struggles slowly upward, propping herself on a pillow. "Jesus. What time is it?"

"Late."

"How was the chef?"

"I liked him. He seems to like the opportunity."

"What about the lease?"

"I'm starting to think we can make it work. I'll show it to you in the morning."

"I have an appointment in the morning," she says, studying me through eyes that grow more alert, more wary by the second. "You look strange."

"I'm excited."

"She was at the interview, wasn't she?"

"Excited about Jambalaya," I say.

Her eyebrows lift. "So you've settled on that name?"

"Whatever we call it," I say, "this is going to be the one."

"The one?"

"The first two were learning experiences. I can't wait to see what happens with the training wheels off."

"That's what I am to you, training wheels?"

"I didn't say that."

She lifts a pillow from my side of the bed and places it on the one already behind her, settling back into the stack. "Can't you concentrate on making the ones we already have as good as can be? Why do we need another?"

"*You* talked me into this business," I say, my voice surprisingly fierce.

"You miss the hyenas over on the Hill?"

"I'm just saying that restaurants are what I do now. What I do, I do to the hilt."

"Restaurants aren't all you do."

"No, but they're what matters."

She looks at me like my face is melting. "Nicholas. Max. Do those names ring a bell?"

"Hank Williams was a father too," I say. "Do people remember him because he made children?"

She nods. "To hell with your children, then. Work on Jambalaya, or whatever you want to call it. If it's really good, some strangers might remember you."

This is the moment when Hank walks downstairs and out the door, stepping into his waiting limousine and cracking open a cold beer. As the car pulls away from the curb, he starts scrawling the first lines of a new song. What I do is go to the bathroom and brush my teeth.

Back in the bedroom, I sit on the corner chair and reach down to untie my shoes. "How was Max's check-up?"

"What do you care?"

"You know I do."

She nods, conceding. "You act like that's a character flaw. If you didn't take an interest in your children, think how many restaurants you'd have."

"The check-up?"

"He's fine. A healthy three-year-old boy."

"Nicholas must be restless. He was in our bed when I came up."

"He does sense things," she says. "Do you?"

"What things?"

"Why can't I look at the lease tomorrow morning?"

I shrug. "You have an appointment."

"With Dr. Shea."

"No wonder," I say, because Dr. Shea's test isn't the first test, or even the second. Dr. Shea's test only confirms the ones taken at home. That's why she's been sleeping so hard.

"No wonder?"

Already on the highway, into his second beer and halfway finished with that new song, Hank misses this moment entirely. This is no kind of moment for Hank. No, this is a moment made to test the mettle of a vain, ambitious, flat-footed performer who lacks the luxury of a limousine.

"No wonder you look so beautiful," I say, and watch what a few friendly words can do. Her color warms, her face opens to me as it hasn't in months.

"Oh, I do not," she says.

On my way to her, I catch sight of the boy who one day, in the middle of his second grade year, will become the eldest of three. How long has he been standing in our bedroom doorway? I go to him, take his shoulders in my hands and gently turn him around, walking with him to his room and peeling the covers back so he can crawl into bed. He lies on his back and I sit on the edge of the bed, stroking his hair. In the nightlight's glow I can see that he's actually looking at me.

"I was wondering," he says, and as I wait for more I press my lips together hard. Harder. "Is this a dangerous place?"

"Dangerous? Why do you ask?"

"I need to know."

"Did something happen to scare you?"

"Nothing happened."

"Did you see something scary?"

"No."

I take his hand. "This is a safe place."

"Cleave Springs?" A hint of challenge in his voice.

"The neighborhood's named after the family that owned all the land before there were houses on it. Cleave, they were called."

"Your dictionary didn't say that."

"My dictionary?"

"Cleave is in there."

"Impressive," I say.

"It means to cut."

"Right. Chefs cut meat with a cleaver."

"And to hold tight."

"Like when we hug."

"Did you know that?" he says.

"Why do you ask?"

"Did you know it before I was born? When you and Mommy moved here?"

"I suppose I did," I say. "But not like I know it now."

He closes his eyes thoughtfully. I watch the surface of his forehead going smooth, like choppy waters when the wind dies. Sometimes, after the pump is primed, this boy will release a great

gush of words. I wait for him to say more, hoping he will, thinking I can be more patient if I don't look at him, so I look everywhere else—the fish tank, the bookshelf, the toy chest, the
chair—before my eyes circle back and find him asleep, his mouth
barely open, the corners raised in a smile that conveys something
I can only read as gratitude, as if he's thanking me for sending
him off to sleep at last, letting him leave me alone in this dangerous place.

When I'm sure he's asleep I remove my hand from his and
tiptoe out of the room. I go into Max's room and pull the covers
up to his chin, standing there to hear him draw and exhale two
healthy breaths before I head out to the hallway and slip down
the stairs.

My briefcase sits on the kitchen table. I take out the lease,
roll it up tightly, and light one end of it at the stove. Afraid of
setting off the smoke alarm, I carry the flaming scroll quickly
out the back door and stand there in the dark yard, convinced,
at least for as long as the flame holds out, that the best work is
done in obscurity.

GOODBYE

DARNELL HATES MOWING the right of way. Teddy knows it. Darnell walks into that dark little office anyway to remind him. "Is it my fault the new cat didn't show?"

Teddy taps away at that computer.

"It can't wait till tomorrow?" Darnell says.

"The right of way's a priority area." Teddy doesn't make the orders, he just gives them. Skinny little white dude, big ears. Light from the screen turns his skin kind of green.

"Don't tell me we goin to the stairway," Darnell says, and watches the color come into those big ears. "I need to take you back there?"

"Look," Teddy says, "I'm desperate. The new guy's AWOL. They been on me three days to get it mowed."

Darnell grumbles across the Parks & Rec yard, all the way out to the truck. He drives over to the north end of Brimslea, where the right of way begins, pulls up to the curb and backs the big riding mower down off the trailer. Section by section, block by block, he mows his way up into his old neighborhood. It's an all-day job. After lunch he reaches the playground section, between Williams and Spring. Mows around the big paved rectangle there, the court where he and his friends used to ball.

Darnell's wide body moved all right back then. He was good at boxing out. Had this sneaky hook shot nobody could block. Held his own on the court, but some of those Cleave Springs boys did a whole lot more than hold their own. Some of them could flat out *play*. Luther Innis, five feet tall on his tiptoes, they called Circles. Dribble circles around anybody. Ramsey Wall had a face only his mama could love—if his mama was blind. Boy got hit with an ugly stick. Someone asked why people called him Pretty, you knew they'd never seen his sweet-ass J.

That was a long time ago. Twenty, twenty-five years? Pavement's still here, but the basketball hoops are long gone. Ten years back, white people started buying the shot-to-hell houses his friends grew up in and spending all kinds of coin to pretty them up. Turned Cleave Springs into a priority area.

Today, while Darnell mows, a crowd of little kids crisscrosses the old basketball court on bikes and scooters and skateboards. The white ones wear helmets. And the black ones, the kids who live down in the Village and pedal up the right of way to get to the nearest playground? Their heads are bare.

Truth is, he's never seen anybody bust their head falling off a bike, but he's seen a few people crash. Ramsey Wall? Took a bullet through the neck. Happened over on Early Street. Darnell didn't watch him hit the pavement, but he was there to lower Pretty's coffin into the ground. Little Luther Innis started knocking down convenience stores for cash to fill his pipe. Only thing he's circling now is a cell. Be an old man when he gets out of Greensville.

But wait a minute. Darnell kills the engine. Wait a damn minute. Like it or not, he's got to mow this right of way. Does that mean he's got to spend all day thinking about a bunch of sad cats from way back? *Hell* no. He can think about whatever—*whoever*—he wants.

From this point on? He's thinking about one cat and one cat only—Ray Bailey, the one they all called Cream. Dude could shoot, pass, handle the ball. Had the whole package, hops included.

Darnell starts the mower again, shaking his head. *Serious* hops.

Ears full of engine noise, nose full of grass smell, he mows on, entertaining himself wondering what might have happened to Cream. Wants to think Cream succeeded, but this takes some finesse. Because if Cream didn't start smoking that crack, if he's not rotting underground or in some penitentiary somewhere, if his body held up, if he developed that left hand, if his luck didn't desert him, if he somehow skyed over all the long odds and landed in the NBA, Darnell would damn sure know about that. So he's got Cream playing in Europe, swingman for some team over there in Italy or France, averaging twelve, fourteen points a game, not pulling down the kind of coin your NBA players command, but doing all right. Darnell's got Cream driving a silver Benz, hooked up with a fine European lady, nice house, three four kids. By now, into his forties, Cream's retired. Unlike Darnell, whose big ass spills over the edges of the mower seat, Cream stays in shape, eats right, still wears the custom tailored suits he did in his playing days. Knees bother him, but you expect that after running the court so long.

Darnell crosses Williams and sets about mowing the dog run section of the right of way. The steep bank on the west side of the run is tricky to mow. If he wants to keep the machine from tipping, keep his ass on the seat, he's got to quit thinking about Cream and concentrate on the job in front of him. He likes the challenge, likes picking his angles, milking the throttle, slicing the turns, making the machine answer him.

That new cat? Take him twice as long to mow the dog run. Give him all day, dude still couldn't cut it this clean.

DINNER IS TWO FILET-O-FISHES, large order of fries and a strawberry shake, extra large. When the food's gone he picks up the phone and calls Texas. Keisha answers.

"What you doin, girl?"

"Sittin here by myself, that's what."

"Where Ray Ray at?"

"Out."

"What about your mama?" Darnell says.

"Out too, lookin for him."

"Lookin for Ray Ray?"

"He got mad and left."

"Why you didn't go with her?"

"Got things to do, that's why. Can you hold on?" He waits while she clicks over to another call. "Daddy," she says, coming back, "that's Janelle about school tomorrow. I better take it."

"What Ray Ray mad about?"

"Do I know? Keep sayin Mama don't respect him."

Darnell chuckles. "Boy, join the club."

"Daddy," she says, "Janelle waitin."

"Go ahead."

"Bye Daddy."

He has a load of laundry to do, work clothes, but wants to watch *Jeopardy* first. Settles down on the couch, back propped on the cushions, feet up on the coffee table, one can of cold beer in his hand and another wedged between the seat cushions. All of the categories up on the board the first round sit outside his comfort zone. He *is* kind of curious how he'll do on U.S. Presidents, though. Learned all of them in school, didn't he?

At the first commercial he yawns, slipping the open beer can down between his thighs. Yawns again, wider.

The knuckles rapping on his door belong to somebody who needs to learn some patience. He hauls himself up off the couch, ambles over to the door and opens it. "Good lord," he says. "Cream."

"I was lookin for you," Cream says, angry. "Went to your house."

Darnell explains that he moved out of the Village a long time ago, before his mother died.

"What you doin in this here cave?"

"Most of my paycheck go to Texas every month. Bikes ain't cheap."

"Helmets ain't either." Cream wears green shorts, a gold jersey with green letters that spell EUROPE. He's back in town, visiting. Wants to ball. They get into the Parks & Rec truck and drive to the right of way, the playground section between Williams and Spring. They walk out onto the court and Cream sees the hoops are gone. He's hot. "What happened here?"

"Didn't want to cut em," Darnell says.

"You cut down the hoops?"

Darnell lowers his eyes.

Cream's voice is somber. "You cut down the hoops."

They walk to one end of the court and stand looking down at the two circular stubs of metal, all that's left of the tall round poles that supported the backboard and rim. Darnell's torch cut them off an inch above the surface of the pavement, leaving two shallow round cups that hold a bit of rain water. He goes down on his hands and knees like a man about to beg or pray. He peers into one of the circles, the still surface of the water reflecting his heavy face. "Least *you* made it," he says, looking over at Cream, who kneels next to him, his smile twisted with mockery.

"That what you believe?"

"What I know," Darnell says. "Cream rises."

"That ain't all cream do."

"It ain't?"

"You know it ain't, man. What else it do?"

When Darnell doesn't answer, Cream stands up and towers over him, glaring. "What else?"

HE WAKES UP with a sour mouth, his body sprawled across the couch, neck sore, beer from the can he didn't finish soaking the leg of his pants. The ten o'clock news is on. He shuts off the TV, shucks his pants and shirt, and goes to bed. Tosses the rest of the night, slipping back to that dream, rolling out of it again, cursing himself for letting Teddy convince him to mow that right of way. Should have said no, left that old murk settled on the bottom of the pond.

Awake half the night, and then he sleeps right through his alarm. Staggers out of bed fifteen minutes before work. No time to shower, no clean work clothes to wear, so he picks up the ones from yesterday and pulls them on.

The pants are still damp when he walks into Teddy's office, a stain on the thigh like he pissed himself. Teddy lifts his eyes from the computer screen and looks him over. "You all right?"

Darnell points at the computer. "That thing any good at findin people?"

"What kind of people you looking for?"

"Cat I used to know. Kid from Cleave Springs."

"He moved away?"

"Don't know what happened to him. One day he was there, next day he wasn't. We never heard."

Teddy reaches for a pen. "Name?"

"Ray Bailey."

Teddy says he'll check it out if he has time.

Darnell is mowing the park by the Triangle today. It's sunny and warm. The damp spot on his pants dries pretty fast, but the smell of stale beer bothers him all day, lingering like that dream, mixing with the stink of the mower and the growing worry over what'll happen if Teddy tracks down Cream. Odds are the dude's dead or incarcerated, which is the kind of information Darnell can do without. But what if things *did* work out for Cream? What if he really played ten twelve years of professional ball? How tickled will he be to hear from a wide-bodied maintenance man who used to bump and grind on the court in the right of way?

When Darnell gets back to the yard, Teddy hands him a slip

of paper with eight or ten phone numbers on it. "I just searched around here. That's the Raymond Baileys. Your guy's probably on there if he stayed local."

Darnell waves the list at Teddy. "How come?"

Teddy nods. "Thanks for mowing the right of way yesterday. Got em off my frickin back."

"Okay," Darnell says, waving the list again, "but don't be thinkin this make that stairway disappear." He watches smiling as Teddy's ears go red.

DINNER IS TWO SIDES of drive-thru chicken, four biscuits, cole slaw, beans, mashed potatoes, extra large Coke. When the food's gone he loads all his work clothes into one of the machines in the laundry room two doors down from his basement unit.

Cracks open a beer and calls Texas.

"What you want, Darnell?" she says after the first ring.

"Hello to you too."

She waits.

"Let me talk to that boy," Darnell says.

"Have to find him first."

"Didn't come home last night?"

"He came home. At eleven damn thirty. Went to school this mornin and I ain't seen him since."

"How come he say you don't respect him?"

She scoffs. "Give to get. That's what I say, Darnell. Want some respect from me? Give it up first."

"When you find him, tell that boy to call me."

"I got a better idea," she says, voice rising. "Come down here and find him your damn self."

The line goes dead and he takes a long drink of beer. Then another. The third one empties the can.

He lifts Teddy's list of numbers from the coffee table and starts staring at it. Stares ten minutes before he tries the first one. A woman, white, says hello and he quickly kills the connection. He tries the next number and it rings a while before an answering machine clicks on. A man's voice, also white, says to leave a message. The third number only rings once before a male voice says hello. Low, but somehow fresh, like it went deep not long ago. Black? White? He's not sure.

"Hello?" the teenage voice says again.

"Ray?"

"You want my dad."

"I'm callin for Ray," Darnell says, flustered. "Ray Bailey."

"Who's calling?" the boy says.

"Name's Darnell."

"Just a minute."

The man who comes onto the phone after the pause has a voice as deep as the boy's, but much more seasoned. "What can I do for you, Darnell?"

"Not sure I got the right Ray Bailey. You the one used to live in Cleave Springs?"

No sound for a minute. "Darnell," the man says, searching. "I only knew one Darnell. He had a nasty hook shot. Couldn't block it if you tried."

Darnell slaps the couch cushion and breaks into a broad grin. "I was a one-trick pony, Cream. You had every shot in the book."

"*Cream.*" The laugh is easy, familiar. "Long time since anybody called me that. We played some ball, Darnell."

"Some *serious* ball."

Dude lives outside Baltimore, it turns out, an hour away. Moved in with his grandparents when he was sixteen. Now he's got his own family up there. Wants to see Darnell, says he'll drive to Cleave Springs and visit the old neighborhood. They agree he should come this Saturday, when Darnell is off. Cream asks where to meet and Darnell flashes back to that dream, when Cream scolded him for living in a cave.

"How about the old court?" Darnell says. "The one in the right of way."

CREAM'S HEAD IS MICHAEL JORDAN-BALD, his skin rich like MJ's, but not as dark. Looks fit, but kind of skinny. Wears a little gold hoop in one ear. A bag with a strap hangs from his shoulder, a big old purse kind of thing that looks like somebody wove it in Guatemala or Peru or someplace like that. Darnell can't picture an NBA player carrying that bag. But who knows, things could be different in Europe.

A heavy grey Saturday, late morning, and not that many kids are playing in the right of way. Darnell and Cream walk around the old court a little bit. Darnell points out the metal stumps.

"No more hoops," Cream says. He lifts his eyes and gazes around at the prettied-up houses on either side of the right of way. "Different place."

"White people moved in, started complainin about this playground. Cops decided to clean it out."

Cream looks back down at the stumps. "You cut them?"

"My job," Darnell says, the memory like the torch he cut with, hot and sharp in the pit of his belly.

They leave the court and walk down the right of way bike path toward Brimslea, Cream throwing out names from way back and Darnell filling him in on what became of the cats they used to run with, none of it any good. When they come to the Village Darnell pauses, looking out from the elevated path over the jumble of sad brick houses, the sagging fences and trash-strewn alleyway.

"This doesn't look so different," Cream says.

"You want to cut over to Shaw?"

Cream shakes his head. "Not really, but I guess I should."

They take the side path down into the Village.

"Chessy," Darnell says as soon as he sees the house, announcing the name he's been trying to think of since they left the right of way path. Place looks about like Darnell remembers. Puke-green door, ratty old plywood porch, windows blocked up with rusty metal screens. "She the one you stayed with here?"

"My aunt," Cream says. "Guy fishing found her six months after I left."

"That's right, in the river. They never did find out who done it to her."

"Maybe I did," Cream says.

Darnell scowls. "Shut up."

"The woman took me in after my mother left. I was eight."

"You kept her together?"

"I don't know," Cream says. "She wasn't in the river *before* my grandparents came and took me." He digs into that purse-looking bag and pulls out a camera with a long black lens that looks dangerous to Darnell, like you could launch little rockets with it. "My kids are always asking me about the place where I grew up.

I never know what to tell them, what to leave out. They wanted to come with me today."

"You said no?"

"Not sure I'm ready to bring them here," Cream says. "I promised to take some pictures, though. Could you get one of me in front of the house?"

He shows Darnell which button to push to make the camera perform. Darnell hoists it. "Old Chessy," he says, finding Cream with his open eye.

"She was all right."

Down in Brimslea, they take a booth at *El Jardin* and order tamales.

"How come they took you?" Darnell says. "Your grandparents."

"They knew where I was headed if I stayed in Cleave Springs. All I knew was basketball."

"How far you go with it, anyway?"

"Basketball?" Cream shakes his head. "Grandpa wouldn't let me go out for the team until I started learning a skill. Something I could still do when my knee blew out. Something I wouldn't have to retire from at 35."

"You found one?"

"Something I liked a whole lot more than basketball." He pats the camera bag and grins. "Not exactly what Grandpa had in mind."

"What you shoot?" Darnell asks.

"People. I do baby pictures, weddings, team pictures—that's

what pays the bills. But I do my own stuff on the side. Show my new work every couple years." He pulls an album with a black cover from his bag and hands it across the table to Darnell. "My family."

These aren't the say-cheese kind of pictures most people take of the family. Cream has shots of his boy and girl watering plants, doing homework, throwing frisbees, brushing teeth, wrestling, sleeping, shouting. He's got his wife, a tall woman with a thick crop of short, slender dreds, playing a trumpet and weeding a flower bed. In most of the shots they pay zero attention to the camera, so used to Cream being there they act like he's not. All the pictures are black and white. The babies from the beginning of the album grow into teenagers by the end.

"Blair's quartet is based in Baltimore," Cream says. "We met in art school. Felice is 17 now, Garrett's 15. What about you?"

"Boy and a girl, just like you."

"How old?" Cream says eagerly.

"Keisha's 11. Ray Ray just turned 14."

"Ray Ray?" Cream fights down a grin. "Should I be flattered?"

Darnell looks at his lap, face all hot. "First couple years, gave me a little thrill every time I said that boy's name. Made me think of you flyin to the rim." He shakes his head. "Never told his mama why I liked it."

"You still with her?"

Darnell looks up. "She down in Texas. Took the kids with her."

"When was that?"

"Two years ago."

"She has people there?"

"Her sister. She done packed off down there with them kids, now she blame me because Ray Ray actin up. Tellin me I should move down there, see if her brother-in-law can get me construction work."

"Not interested?"

"I'm a quit my job and go down to Texas for a *see-if?*"

"You see them much?"

Darnell shakes his head. "Send a check down there every month. Talk to em on the phone when they got time for me."

Cream pulls his wallet out of the Guatemala bag and puts money on the table.

"I can pay," Darnell says, shoving the bills away.

Cream smiles. "Sure you can. Let me this time."

The cutting-torch flares down in Darnell's belly again. He grips both sides of the table. "Put that money away."

Cream lifts his eyebrows and scoops up the bills.

OUT ON THE SIDEWALK, Darnell tries to ease the vibe. "Back in the hood," he says, clapping Cream on the shoulder.

Cream nods. "You're about the only one still here. How'd that happen?"

"'You got work, you know who you is.' What my mama used to say."

"Your daddy worked in the railyard?"

"Till they shut it up. That's when *he* forgot who he was."

On the right of way bike path, a white couple approaches,

both wearing tank tops, skimpy shorts, and flashy training shoes. They smile as they whisk past.

"How long you been with Parks & Rec?" Cream says.

"Ten years, give or take."

"You wear a uniform?"

"That's right."

"What's it look like?"

"Pants and shirt, khaki green. Name patch up here on the breast pocket. Why?"

"A lot of people think black men are lazy," Cream says. "But you know what? I work for a living. Everywhere I go, I see black men working. I'm shooting a series called 'Working Man'."

"You want *my* picture?"

"If I could," Cream says. "What I'd like to do is shoot you in that uniform, with the tools of your trade."

"Tools?"

"That's right," Cream says, patting his camera bag. "Tools express the worker. Is there some tool you use the most? Something you're really skilled with?"

Darnell chews on it a minute. "Ain't nobody handle them big mowers like I do. That's my specialty."

"Where do they keep the mowers?"

"Got em in a yard. Locked up on Saturday."

"You have the key?"

Darnell shakes his head. "I know who do."

CREAM DRIVES AND DARNELL TELLS HIM where to turn. On the way to Teddy's they talk over the shoot some more. Cream wants to do it in the right of way playground so he can get some shots of the old court. Normally Darnell wouldn't go for this, on account of all the people. But the heavy morning has turned into a hot and humid afternoon. The playground should be deserted.

Teddy lives in one half of a little brick duplex. He's out front mowing his lawn when they pull up to the curb. The sight makes Darnell smile. He gets out of the car and Teddy kills the engine before walking over. "Something wrong?"

"You still remember how to cut grass?"

Teddy glances back at his lawn. "Like riding a bike."

"Got a favor to ask you," Darnell says, and explains what he wants Teddy to do.

Teddy shakes his head. "Can't let you take my keys to the yard, Darnell. No way."

"Come with me, then. Open the yard yourself."

"And then what, let you haul a mower over to the right of way? On a Saturday? I can't do that." He flicks his face to the side and spits, an old outdoor habit of his that Darnell instantly remembers.

"Tell you what," Darnell says. "That stairway? Do this for me, I won't take you back there no more. That's a promise."

Teddy already had a decade at Parks & Rec back when Darnell got hired. They crewed together two years before Teddy got promoted to his indoor job, but they only ever went drinking once. The day the right of way hoops came down, Teddy watched Darnell do the cutting and afterward offered to buy him a drink. Darnell was thirsty for some alcohol, but not if he had to drink it in a bar full of white dudes. He told Teddy he'd go, but only if he got to pick the place. Teddy got plastered that night, chasing beers with Jack Daniel's shots and then swaying through a barroom full of black people, bumping into folks and singing "Stairway to Heaven" at the top of his lungs. Darnell saved Teddy from getting punched out six or seven times before he drove him home and put his drunk ass in bed.

"Let me put this mower in back," Teddy says.

DARNELL RIDES SHOTGUN in Cream's Camry, and Teddy rides in back. At Darnell's apartment, Cream and Teddy wait in the car while Darnell changes into clean work clothes. The next stop is the yard, where Teddy unlocks the gate and then hops around like he's got jumping beans in his shorts, whipping his head this way and that, worrying somebody will catch them in the act. Darnell fires up a truck with a mower already loaded on its trailer, and rolls out through the open gate. Teddy locks the gate behind and then climbs into the shotgun seat.

Darnell creeps along until he sees the Camry in his rearview. "Like old times," he says, speeding up. Teddy just shakes his head.

The playground is deserted, like Darnell hoped. Cream wants to get Darnell and the mower and most of the court in the same shot. He scouts around a bit before deciding to shoot from a bench that sits at midcourt, a few feet back from the edge of the pavement. He stands on the bench while Darnell drives the mower down off the trailer and maneuvers it into position on the court. The engine killed, he sits hot and silent as Cream shoots and talks.

"I'm liking this wide angle, Darnell. Gives me a lot of the

court, with you in the middle on that mower—past and present, work and play, know what I mean? I'm coming in close now, Darnell. Got the zoom on you, brother, got your name patch and your face." He steps down off the bench and starts to circle Darnell, shooting him from all sides, kneeling down, standing up tall, gliding around the way he used to do on this court, his patter never stopping, the shots clicking in a steady rhythm.

Darnell imagines he can see the developed images as fast as Cream shoots them, the pictures spreading out in lines across the coffee table while he sits there trying to pick out one, maybe a couple, to stick in the envelope with his next check.

When Cream finishes, he says there's one last shot he'd like to get before they leave and calls Teddy over to help. He leads Darnell and Teddy to the end of the court where one of the hoops used to stand. When the camera's ready he hands it to Teddy, saying all he's got to do is get him and Darnell in the frame and push the button. "Now Darnell, let's you and me kneel down here by these pole stumps. I want this for Felice and Garrett, so I can show them my old home boy Darnell and tell them how we used to ball."

Teddy snaps four shots before he gets one Cream likes. Afterward, Cream asks Teddy how long he's been Darnell's supervisor.

"Seven eight years," Teddy says.

"You the one made him cut down these hoops?"

Teddy shakes his head. "That was back when me and Darnell rode together. Boss gave us that order and I told Darnell I'd cut them poles down. Didn't think he'd want to."

Cream turns to Darnell. "You *wanted* to?"

Darnell nods.

"Why?"

"Where was Pretty?" Darnell says. "Pretty was in the cemetery. Where was Circles? Locked up in jail. Where was Cream? Busy takin pictures of his trumpet-playin wife. Where was Darnell? Right here, that's where. Ain't nobody came and rescued *me* up out of Cleave Springs. I was right here, watchin em pull it apart, house by house, block by block. Cleanin us out. Those was *our* hoops," he says, glaring at Cream. "I'm a let Teddy cut em?"

"You can leave too," Teddy says.

Darnell looks over. "What you talkin about?"

Teddy flicks his head to the side and spits. "You don't have to stay."

"Where you think I should go, Tahiti? Maybe I'll go to Miami Beach."

"I watched you cut down them hoops," Teddy says. "Never saw nobody so tore up over a thing. Why you think I got so drunk that night? Why you think I squirm every time you remind me?"

"Ain't you embarrassed?"

"Because I couldn't hold my liquor and acted like a fool? Maybe for a few days, but not no more." Teddy shakes his head, remembering. "What gets me is the look on your face. That was some suffering."

The heat in Darnell's belly rises up like a mushroom cloud inside him. A hot, weird gust blows through his head. He drops to his knees.

"Teddy's right," Cream says. "What about Texas?"

Sweat pours off Darnell's head, running down under his collar onto his chest and back. "Ain't nothin for me down there."

"They need you," Cream says.

"They need my money."

"That boy needs *you*. Ray Ray does."

His son's name, released over the old court, shreds Darnell's defense. Sobs start to slam him like body punches. Wails pour up out of him and into the thick heat. He tears at his shirt buttons, sits back on his haunches and moans. Then he doubles over and weeps, holding his big wet face in his hands.

Eventually his noises start to settle and he can hear neighborhood sounds. A passing car, a bark. He breathes raggedly still, his eyes shut. A hand touches his shoulder and he opens his eyes to Teddy offering a handkerchief. He takes the fragile white cloth and drags it across his brow. Cream is next to him too. He reaches down and takes one of Darnell's arms. Teddy takes the other arm and the two men help him to his feet.

Darnell wavers, shaking his head. "You wanted a picture of a workin man."

Cream smiles. "What I just saw? Would've been a whole series by itself, if Teddy let me shoot it."

Darnell looks over at Teddy. Dude's arms are crossed, his mouth all hard. "Give a guy some frickin privacy. Jesus."

Cream closes his eyes and nods. "He's right. Would've made one hell of a series, though."

"What would you call it?" Darnell asks.

"That's easy," Cream says. "I'd call it 'Goodbye'."